SECRETS IN THE FIRE

SECRETS
IN THE
FIRE

Henning Mankell

ANNICK PRESS

TORONTO + NEW YORK + VANCOUVER

We acknowledge the support of the Canada Council for the Arts, the Ontario Arts Council,
and the Government of Canada through the Book Publishing Industry Development
Program (BPIDP) for our publishing activities.

Cover design by Irvin Cheung/iCheung Design
Cover illustration by Farida Zaman
Interior design by Tanya Lloyd Kyi

CATALOGUING IN PUBLICATION DATA

Mankell, Henning, 1948-
    Secrets in the fire / written by Henning Mankell ; translated by Anne Connie
Stuksrud. — North American ed.

Translation of: Eldens hemlighet.

ISBN 1-55037-801-5 (bound). — ISBN 1-55037-800-7 (pbk.)

    I. Stuksrud, Anne Connie II. Title.

PZ7.M298Se 2003   839.73'74   C2003-900340-X

The text was typeset in Apollo.

Distributed in Canada by:	Distributed in the U.S.A. by:	Published in the U.S.A. by
Firefly Books Ltd.	Firefly Books (U.S.) Inc.	Annick Press (U.S.) Ltd.
66 Leek Crescent	P.O. Box 1338	
Richmond Hill, ON	Ellicott Station	
L4B 1H1	Buffalo, NY 14205	

Printed and bound in Canada

Visit us at **www.annickpress.com**

In memory of Maria Alface...

an African girl
who died when she was very young.

This book is about her sister,
Sofia,
who survived.

A FEW WORDS BEFORE YOU READ THIS BOOK...

THERE ARE MANY expressive and beautiful words in the Swedish language.

One of these words is *okuvlig:* indomitable.

When you say it out loud you can get a sense of what it means...

That you won't let yourself be trampled on.

That you won't give in.

This book is about an indomitable person called Sofia. She exists in real life and lives in one of the poorest countries in the world: Mozambique, on the east coast of Africa.

Mozambique was once a rich country. But it became poor as the result of a war which raged there for almost twenty years. Prior to 1974, Mozambique was a Portuguese colony. When the country became independent and went its own way, there were many who tried to prevent it—in particular the wealthy Portuguese who had lost their previous power. Many of them moved to South Africa. Racists in South Africa didn't like what was going on in neighboring

Mozambique, either. They gave money and weapons to poverty-stricken and discontented Mozambicans, and encouraged them to initiate civil war. And, as happens in all wars, it was the civilians who suffered the most. Many people died and many fled. Sofia was one of these. But she survived.

This book is about Sofia and the things that happened to her. Things that changed her whole life.

HENNING MANKELL

This is my story
as I want it to be kept alive
in your memory.

The African heart
is like the sun—
big, red,
a blood-colored piece of silk.

The African dusk dances.
Out of the rising sun
grow the first sounds,
first whispering, murmuring
and then, at last, much stronger.

But it is still night.
And Sofia is dreaming...

CHAPTER ONE

SOFIA IS RUNNING through the night. It's dark and she's terrified.

She doesn't know why she's running, why she's scared, or where she's going.

But there's something behind her, something deep in the darkness that frightens her. She knows she has to go faster, she has to run faster. Whatever the invisible thing behind her is, it's getting closer and closer. She's frightened and alone and all she can do is run.

She's running along a path that twists between low trees and thornbushes. She can't see the path, but she knows it by heart. Her feet know where the path turns and where it is straight. It's the path she walks along every morning with her sister, Maria, that leads out to the field where they grow maize and greens and onions. Every morning at dawn she walks along it, and every night, just before dusk, she and Maria return with their Mama Lydia to the hut where they all live.

But why is she running there now, in the darkness of the night?

What is it that hunts her in the darkness—a beast with no eyes? She can feel its breath on her neck, and she tries to run even faster.

But she doesn't have the strength. Her first thought is to hide. To get off the path, to curl up and shrink into the bushes. She leaps the way she's seen the antelopes leap, and leaves the ground.

Then she realizes.

That's exactly what the beast in the darkness wants her to do—leave the path: the most dangerous thing of all.

Every morning Mama Lydia would say: *Never leave the path. Not even by a step. Never take shortcuts. Promise me that.*

She knows there's something dangerous in the ground. Armed soldiers that no one can see. Buried in the ground, invisible. Waiting and waiting for a foot to step on them. She tries desperately to keep hovering in the air. She knows she mustn't put her feet back on the ground. But she hasn't got the strength to keep hovering—she hasn't got wings like a bird—and she's being pulled towards the ground and the soles of her feet are already touching the dry earth.

Then she wakes up.

She's wet with sweat, her heart hammers in her

chest, and at first she doesn't know where she is. But then she hears the breathing of her sleeping brother and mother. They're lying close to each other on the floor of the hut.

She reaches out carefully and touches her mother's back. Her mother stirs, but doesn't wake.

Sofia lies with open eyes in the silence and the dark. Mama Lydia's breathing is light and irregular, as if she were already awake and preparing the porridge for their morning meal. On her left side is Alfredo.

Before too long there will be another person sleeping on the floor of the hut. Mama Lydia is due to have a baby soon. Sofia has seen her fat before. She knows there can't be many days to go.

She thinks about her dream. Now that she's woken up, she's both relieved and happy, but she's also sad.

She thinks about her dream—and about what happened that morning one year ago.

She thinks about Maria, whose breathing she can no longer hear in the darkness.

Maria, who is gone.

Sofia lies awake in the darkness for a long time. An owl hoots somewhere outside, and a wary rat rustles outside the straw wall of the hut.

She thinks about what happened that morning, when everything was as it used to be, and she and

Maria were on their way to help Lydia weed the fields on the outskirts of the village.

And she thinks about all the things that happened before then.

CHAPTER TWO

IT WAS OLD MUAZENA who told Sofia and Maria about the secrets in the fire.

Every flame has a secret, she told them. If you sit at the right distance from the fire, you can look so deeply into the dancing flames that you can foresee what is going to happen in the future, in the days that lie stretched out and unused ahead of you. Muazena had pointed her wrinkled, shaking old hand towards a field where the plants stood in rows.

"That's how life looks," said Muazena. "Every day is a plant that you should nurse and water, keep clear of weeds, and one day harvest. Every plant represents a day in your life that you haven't yet lived."

All memories are found in the fire, too.

Old Muazena had told Sofia and Maria about that as well, when they were still quite young. By looking into the fire you could unlock memories that you might have thought you had forgotten forever.

Sofia often thought of Muazena. But Muazena wasn't around now, any more than Maria was. When

Sofia thought about Muazena she went back to the time before they had been forced to flee. That was before the long journey, before they settled to live here by the river. Those had been good times, when she barely knew what pain was. Or sadness. Or hunger. Or the worst of them all: loneliness.

What Sofia remembered most clearly was the village of round huts with their neatly flattened roofs of palm leaves. They had lived in that village all their lives. That was where she had been born, and where Maria and Alfredo had been born. When she was a baby, her father, Hapakatanda, had lifted her towards the sky to let her greet the sun. She'd been tied to her mother's back—her mother Lydia, who at the time had been the prettiest and strongest woman in the whole village. Sofia used to be on Lydia's back as she bent forward to hoe the dry soil. She always heard music when she thought of that time: drums and the monotonous melody of the timbila. Sofia still kept an echo inside her of the rocking movement her mother made when she danced with the other women. Sofia couldn't remember that she'd ever been hungry then.

Or scared. It had been a happy time.

Muazena had said something about that, too.

She'd been talking about paradise. She'd said: *Happiness is what we realize we have had, after we've lost it.*

Then it had happened—and Sofia had been trying to forget it ever since. But the memory was like a scar on her skin that would never go away.

It was night.

No moon, no stars.

Then suddenly her whole life exploded. A sharp white light filled the hut and then there was a series of powerful cracks. It was the one memory in her life that she most wanted to forget. She had seen twisted faces in the sharp light. They were humans, but they looked like monsters, and she knew right away that they had come to kill her and everyone else in the village.

They were bandits.

They had sneaked towards the village under cover of darkness and burned the huts and killed the people. In the chaos of fire and death that followed—the bleeding bodies, the screaming and shouting— Hapakatanda had tried to shield Sofia and Maria. But he was struck by the blade of a large knife, or maybe it had been an axe, and he'd fallen across them, so that Sofia and Maria lay hidden underneath him.

Afterwards, everything was silent.

That was when Sofia knew what was meant by the Silence of Death. But her father had managed to do in death what he'd been trying to do before he died: protect her and Maria from the knives and axes and guns.

In the morning, when the sun returned, they dared to crawl out. Their father was dead and they were crying. Muazena was dead, too. She lay face down in the dying fire. But Lydia wasn't anywhere to be found, nor was Alfredo. Neither Sofia nor Maria dared to call out, and they wept soundlessly as they crept from the hut. They went through the village. Dead people lay all over the place—everyone they knew and were related to, people they had played with, worked with, laughed with. The monsters who had come during the night had brought with them the Silence of Death. They had turned the village into a cemetery. People lay everywhere in twisted positions. The bandits had even killed the dogs. Some people had their arms and legs cut off, some even had their heads cut off. The girls walked through the dead village, through the Silence of Death, until they reached the last of the burned huts. Sofia was sure that Lydia and Alfredo would be somewhere. Not everyone could be dead. She and Maria couldn't be the only ones left. Muazena once told them that the biggest disaster that could happen to anyone was to be the very last person left on earth.

"I don't want to be the last person," Sofia thought, weeping. "If something happens to Maria, I'll be left here alone."

Lydia was alive. So was Alfredo. Sofia and Maria

found them on the outskirts of the village, hidden in the bushes. There were Lydia, Alfredo, two other women, and three children. Sofia and Maria didn't cry out with relief because the bandits might still be around to hear them. They all just held each other close and lay hidden all day in the bushes, without water and without food, waiting for it to get dark.

Then they fled. At first they walked through the prickly scrub under cover of night. After a while they dared to travel during the day as well. Since they didn't know which way to go, they simply went straight ahead, straight across the dry countryside towards the high mountains that showed on the horizon. Sofia could still remember now how hungry she had been. But it was thirst that really had plagued her.

On the third day, Lydia argued with the other women about which direction they should go. Lydia, Sofia, Maria, and Alfredo continued towards the mountains while the others went a different way.

They kept walking and never looked back.

Somewhere on that road towards the unknown an old woman appeared suddenly in front of them. She was very poor; her clothes hung in tatters and her legs were swollen and covered in sores. Sofia thought she must have been as old as Muazena. When Mama Lydia spoke to her they understood each other, since their languages were similar. Lydia told her what had happened.

"It was bandits. They came during the night and they killed my husband."

"Anyone else?" the old woman asked. "The bandits are monsters and they never kill just the one. They kill as many as they can."

"They killed everyone in the village," Lydia answered.

"And the dogs," said Sofia. "They killed all the dogs, too."

The old woman started to rock her body, tossing her head from side to side and wailing. Lydia did the same, and then Sofia, Maria, and Alfredo joined in. They rocked their bodies back and forth, and now at last they dared to shriek aloud their sorrow and pain, for all to hear.

Then they continued towards the mountains. The old woman followed them and shared some meat from a dead bird. They found water to drink in an almost-dry riverbed.

By night they slept next to fires underneath mighty baobab trees. Sofia would wake Maria when she heard lions growling in the darkness.

The old woman never told them her name. But she had a friendly smile—despite having lost all her teeth.

The monsters returned in Sofia's dream that night. When one of them lifted the axe over her father, she woke up. Lydia was sleeping with Alfredo huddled close to her body. The old woman slept next to the dying coals of the fire, with Maria beside her. Sofia wondered whether it could be the spirit of Muazena who walked again in the old woman who never gave her name.

They continued their journey towards the mountains in the early dawn. The mountains seemed to be just as far away as they were when they set out. Sofia heard Mama Lydia ask the old woman about the city.

"I've never been there," said the old woman.

"Is it far away?" Lydia asked.

"The city is far away, so that people like you and me and your children can't get there. My legs are old and aching, your children's legs are too short and young. None of us have legs made to walk to the city."

Lydia didn't ask any more questions. They continued in silence. The heat was intense. They tried to shade themselves from the sun by wrapping parts of their *capulanas,* the colorful pieces of fabric they wore as dresses, around their heads. The old woman still had some water left in a dirty plastic cup. But by late afternoon they still hadn't seen any clumps of trees, which would signal water close by.

Just as the brief hour of dusk arrived, the old woman suddenly stopped and, with great difficulty, sat down on the dry ground.

"I've come this far," she said after a moment of silence. "And now I've finished walking."

Lydia told Sofia and Maria to collect wood for a fire.

"But there aren't any trees," said Sofia. "Where are we going to sleep?"

"Do as I tell you," Lydia replied, and her voice sounded tired. "We're staying here tonight."

Sofia wanted to ask more. Who was going to protect them against the wild animals? What would happen if the fire burned out and there was no tree-spirit to guard them? But she didn't dare to ask any more questions. She'd heard in Mama Lydia's voice that she didn't have any answers right now. Along with Maria and Alfredo, Sofia collected dry grass and sticks. She kept herself close to Alfredo the whole time. There could have been snakes, and he was still too small to understand when to be afraid.

They lit the fire and Sofia saw that the old woman was sitting motionless, with her eyes open.

"Isn't she going to eat anything?" Sofia asked as they ate the last of the dried meat.

"She isn't hungry," Lydia answered.

"Isn't she going to sleep?" Sofia asked softly when they'd curled up next to the fire.

"She's already sleeping," Lydia replied. "Don't ask any more questions. Sleep."

The next day at dawn, when Sofia woke up, the old woman was still sitting in the same position.

Her body was completely stiff. Sofia knew that now she too was dead.

She roused Lydia, who woke up at once.

"She's dead," said Sofia.

Lydia rose and went over to the old woman. She looked at her silently. Then she woke Maria and Alfredo and told Sofia to bring the old woman's plastic cup.

When they'd been walking for some time, Sofia turned around. She could see the old woman like a distant shadow. Maybe she'd already turned into one of the twisted, dead roots that lay spread about on the dry, red ground.

Sofia had many questions. She wondered why she'd been forced into this world of the dead.

If only I could reach the high mountains, she thought. Beyond them there must be living people.

They walked for a long time, for several days. Later, when Sofia looked back on that time, it seemed like a dream. Maybe it had been—maybe it was possible to travel in your dreams? Maybe you could climb over mountains and wade through half-dry rivers without waking up?

But at night the twisted faces returned. The monsters would lean over her and she would wake with a jerk. Then they would retreat. But they were always somewhere close by, she knew that. They watched her but she couldn't see them.

They walked for many days.

Sofia asked Lydia where they were going.

"Away," Lydia answered. "Away from those who killed Hapakatanda and your relatives."

Sofia tried to believe that what Lydia called "Away" was a place, maybe a village, that was already there waiting for them. But she also knew that she had no excuse to be so childish, since she was no longer small enough to be carried on her mother's back. Away was away, nowhere.

One day Sofia saw the ocean for the first time.

They had walked up a hill. It was late afternoon, and Sofia's feet were swollen and sore.

Then she saw the ocean. It was like river without a bank on the other side: a lake in shining turquoise that no bridge could cross. Sofia had never seen the ocean, but she immediately felt as though she had come home. There was something familiar to be found in the unknown, after all. Maybe she had now discovered one of those secrets that Muazena had told her about, one of the secrets in the fire. Perhaps all those who were driven from their homes by bandits or monsters had another kingdom waiting for them? The important thing was to avoid sitting down as the old woman had done—because just when you think you have run out of your last bit of energy, you might arrive at the home you didn't even know you had.

They walked down to the beach. The sand was different, softer under their feet. Lydia sat in the shade, under a tree by the shore. Sofia and Maria ran down to the water together. It was salty when they tasted it. They waded out until they heard Lydia shouting at them to be careful.

Afterwards, Sofia asked whether they had now arrived.

Lydia shook her head.

"How would we live here?" she asked. "How could we get anything to grow in sand? How could we plant anything in the ocean? We have to keep going."

The next day, when they continued their journey and were walking inland again, Sofia kept turning around to look at the endless, shimmering water. She would never forget the ocean.

After a long time, they reached a village where Lydia's husband Hapakatanda had some distant relatives. The town's leader, an old man who was almost blind, told them they could stay. They built a small hut of straw and clay on the outskirts of the village, and in the mornings Lydia, Sofia, and Maria went with the other women to work in the fields.

But one day a man came running to tell them that a neighboring town had been attacked by bandits the previous night. The same afternoon everyone fled the village with their children and their goats. They hid for more than a month, in constant fear of the bandits finding them. They had almost nothing to eat, only roots and the lizards and rats they managed to catch.

During this time Alfredo was seriously ill. Sofia thought he was going to die, too. When a child started shivering with cold even though the sun was hot, she knew that Death had blown its dangerous breath through his nostrils. But Alfredo recovered.

When the villagers decided to return to their homes, Lydia said that she and the children wouldn't go with them, but would continue their journey.

"Where are we going?" Sofia asked.

"To where there are no bandits."

"Where is that?" Sofia asked.

"I don't know. Don't ask so many questions."

Sofia was constantly afraid that her mother would do what the old woman had done: sit herself down on the ground and stiffen into a tree root. Then Sofia would be alone with Maria and Alfredo, and she wouldn't know where to find a home. Every night when they set up camp, Sofia would secretly watch her mother. Was she going to sit down and go rigid?

Sofia felt surrounded by fear. The bandits were both behind and in front of her. Every time Lydia didn't sit down and stiffen into a tree root, Sofia was scared it would happen the day after.

But it didn't happen.

And then one day the long journey ended.

They came to a village made up entirely of people who had fled the bandits. They all spoke different languages. A white man who was a priest looked at them sadly. With help from a man who spoke her language, Lydia explained where they'd run from. She told about the night when the bandits had come to plunder, burn, and kill.

"Even the dogs," said Sofia. "They even killed our dogs."

For the second time they found a clearing and built a hut of straw and clay. A river rippled not far below it.

The first night they spent under a roof again, Sofia lay looking out at the darkness. She noticed that Maria, who was lying next to her, hadn't fallen asleep either.

"This is where we're going to live," Sofia whispered.

"Why don't the bandits come here?" asked Maria.

"They might not be able to find their way," Sofia answered. "Think of how many days we've been walking. Our feet are swollen and covered in sores."

"The bandits might have shoes," Maria said. Sofia could hear that she was frightened.

"I don't think the bandits have shoes," Sofia said. "We're going to live here. Nothing is going to happen to us."

Maria moved closer. Sofia could feel the warmth of Maria's body against her own.

This is where we're going to live, she thought. But I'll never see my father Hapakatanda again. Nor any of the others who were my friends and my family. I won't see the dogs again, either.

Suddenly she realized she was crying. It was as though she hadn't dared to feel the grief she carried inside until now. If all the sorrow she felt had been put in a basket for her to carry on her head, she would have collapsed. She was too small to carry such a heavy burden.

Still, she knew she had no choice. It would always be there, the basket of sorrows, throughout her whole life.

Finally she fell asleep and dreamed about Muazena and the secrets in the fire.

"We've arrived," she whispered to Muazena in her dream. "We've arrived and we're still alive. And I've seen the ocean."

The next day Sofia woke early, but Lydia was up already. When Sofia came out of the hut, rubbing the sleep from her eyes, Lydia was squatting down making a fire. She looked up at Sofia and smiled. Sofia thought of how long it was since she had seen Lydia smiling. It filled her with happiness. She knew now that the long journey was over.

They had finally arrived.

Here they would begin to live their lives again.

CHAPTER THREE

ONE DAY, when Sofia was sweeping around the hut and Maria had gone to fetch water from the river, Lydia called out to her. She was crushing corn with a stick and needed to stretch her back.

"You and Maria look so much alike," she said and laughed. "Not even I can always tell you apart. Yet you're not twins."

"Which one am I?" Sofia asked.

"Of course, now I can see that you're Sofia," Lydia said. "But sometimes I'm unsure who's who, even though there's a whole year between you. Maria will always be a year older than you."

Then she went on crushing the corn with the thick, heavy stick.

Sofia kept sweeping and thought about what Lydia had said. She thought it was strange that a person couldn't catch up with someone else. Everything else in the world that she knew about could. Corn plants sooner or later reached similar height, tomatoes the same redness, chickens the same size. But not people. Not her and Maria.

She saw Maria coming along the path from the lake with the heavy water bucket on her head. Sofia put aside the broom and hoped Lydia wouldn't notice she was sneaking away. Lydia didn't approve of people leaving their work before it was finished. Maria would never do that, Sofia thought. She would finish sweeping. There, at least, is a difference between us.

Maria was grimacing because of the heavy bucket on her head. Sofia helped her put it down. They carried the bucket between them up to the hut. Meanwhile, Sofia told Maria what Lydia had been saying.

"When we have children they might look like each other, too," Maria said.

"That probably depends on who their papas are," Sofia answered. "The reason we look so alike is because we both look like Hapakatanda."

Then she almost bit her tongue. Horrified, she realized she'd done something you should never do: she'd mentioned their dead father.

Maria signaled that she wanted to put the bucket down. Then she sat on the ground, and Sofia did the same.

"I dream about Papa every night," Maria said. "I dream that it's morning and he's sitting outside the hut."

"You know that he's dead," Sofia answered. "The bandits killed him with an axe."

"Then why do I dream he's alive?"

Sofia didn't have an answer. Most of the time it was Maria who asked the questions and Sofia who answered. It should really have been the other way around, since Maria was the oldest and ought to have known more.

But now Sofia didn't have any answers.

"Are we always going to live here?" Maria asked, and Sofia could tell she was sad all of a sudden. She was huddled up as if she had a pain somewhere in her body.

"I don't know," said Sofia. "But one day when we grow up, perhaps we can go back home. Even if Lydia stays here."

"How will we find home?"

"It'll work somehow. If we wish for it strongly enough, we'll find our way back."

They sat talking for a while beside the water bucket. They promised each other that no matter what happened they would one day return home to the village that the bandits had burned down.

When they arrived at the hut carrying the water bucket between them, Lydia was angry. She talked fast and loud and pointed at the broom and told Sofia that a real woman would have finished sweeping before she put the broom away. Sofia didn't say anything. She knew Lydia was never angry for long.

But neither Sofia nor Maria forgot what they'd talked about beside the water bucket.

One day they would go back home. That was a promise neither of them was allowed to break.

They'd built their hut and they had a new home. But for a long time everything remained unfamiliar and strange. It was difficult living in a village where no one knew each other or spoke the same language. In the beginning, both Sofia and Maria were shy of the other villagers. But they were lucky because they found one friend almost right away—a boy called Lino, who was a couple of years older than they were. He lived in a hut nearby, along the dusty road which led to the house where the white priest and the two nuns lived. Lino spoke the same language as Maria and Sofia. He was tall and thin. But the remarkable thing about him was that he was cross-eyed. He could look at both Maria and Sofia at the same time.

One day, there he was, standing outside their hut. It was a Sunday and they weren't working out in the fields. His clothes were just as ragged as everyone else's. He had a shoe on one of his feet. As he owned only that one shoe, he had painted a shoe on the other foot. Lydia had gone to try and get a bar of soap by trading a basket she'd been weaving in the evenings, and Maria and Sofia were home alone, looking after Alfredo.

"How is it that you look so much alike?" Lino asked. "You can use each other as a mirror."

Sofia thought she ought to reply, but she couldn't think of anything to say.

"How can you look in two directions at the same time?" she finally said.

"That's my secret," Lino answered.

Then he told them that he'd come to the village with an aunt and uncle. His parents had been kidnapped by bandits in an attack far, far away. He didn't even know if they were still alive. Maria told him what had happened in their village.

"We saw the ocean," Sofia said. "Have you seen the ocean?"

Lino shook his head.

"I'm going to travel all over the world one day," he said. "And I'll be seeing twice as much as everyone else."

Then he told them about the school. The white priest and the two nuns had an educational program for the kids in the village. They wanted all of them to come every day to learn how to read and write and do sums.

"We don't have any money," said Sofia, who really wanted to go to school.

"We have to work with our mama," said Maria.

"It doesn't cost anything," Lino said. "Do you think I've got any money? Would I be wearing one shoe if I had money?"

"It won't work anyway," Maria said. "We have to work. How else would we eat?"

"School is only in the afternoons," Lino said. "Three hours a day. I can almost read already."

Later, when Lino left, the sisters sat in the shade at the back of the house.

"I don't think he spoke the truth," Maria said. "A school can't be free. And besides, we only have ragged clothes. I don't think you can go to school if your clothes aren't whole."

"The most important thing is that you're not dirty," Sofia said. "I don't think he lied. Why would he have done that?"

"It won't work anyway," Maria said. "We have to help Lydia. Who's going to look after Alfredo while we're in school? We can't take him with us."

"We could maybe go one day each," said Sofia hesitantly.

"And learn every second letter?" asked Maria. "And every second number?"

They kept talking it over, back and forth, and completely forgot about Alfredo. Neither of them had ever dreamed they would be able to go to school. There had been no school in their old village. Only the village secretary, who'd gone to a missionary school, could read and write. He was the one who had written the letters anyone in town needed to write, and he was the one who read out the various messages from the governor and other important people.

Was it really possible that they could go to school? If that were so, Sofia thought, their having run away wasn't a totally bad thing. Something positive might come out of it after all.

She had seen the ocean.

She might be able to go to school.

However, it could never make up for the fact that Hapakatanda, Muazena, and their relatives were dead. It couldn't even make up for the fact that the bandits had killed their dogs.

But, even so, it was something.

"Alfredo!" Maria exclaimed suddenly and jumped up. Lydia was always afraid he might drown in the river or be swallowed by a crocodile. She was also scared a snake might bite him. The girls rushed around the side of the house. But then they relaxed; Alfredo had fallen asleep beside the wall. Dust was blowing across his face and, in his sleep, he brushed at a fly that was trying to crawl into his nose.

Lydia returned late in the afternoon with a bar of soap. First they went down to the river to wash. While two of them looked out for crocodiles, the third one washed. Then they swapped around. Lydia was in a good mood. She stood half-naked in the water, singing as she lathered herself.

"We'll talk to her tonight," Maria said. "When she's singing she's in a good mood. But you'll have to ask her."

"Me?" Sofia said with surprise. "You're the oldest."

"You're better at talking," Maria said. "And since I'm the oldest, I decide. You'll ask Mama."

At dusk they were sitting around the plates of maize porridge and greens, helping themselves to food with their fingers and eating in silence. Maria looked at Sofia and frowned, signaling that now was the time to speak. Mama Lydia never sat still or idle for long. After the meal, she would start preparing for the night immediately, rolling out the thin quilts they slept on and arranging the *capulanas* they covered themselves with.

"There's a school here," Sofia said. "It's free. You can learn to read and write and do sums. It's only in the afternoons."

Lydia looked at her in surprise.

"Why are you telling me this?" she asked.

Sofia closed her eyes and braced herself.

To ask something difficult was like trying to make a huge leap.

"Maria and I would like to start school," she said.

Lydia finished chewing and wiped her fingers before she answered.

"You don't have to worry yourselves about going to school," she said. "You already work hard in the cornfields. I don't want to force you into doing more than you have to."

"But we want to," Sofia said.

Lydia looked at her in amazement, and then looked with as much amazement at Maria.

"You don't have to know how to read and write in order to weed a field," she said. "You don't need to know how to do sums to hoe and plant seeds."

Sofia didn't know what to say. How could she make her mother understand that they wanted something more? To be able to read what was written on a sign, to be able to write their own names.

"The white priest wants all the children to go to school," she finally said. "Maybe we should obey him."

Sofia knew that her mother had a lot of respect for white people. In their old village, everyone had been like that. When a white man or woman said something, you always had to listen carefully. Sofia didn't know why. At one time, the white people had been in charge of their country, but it wasn't like that anymore. The only one she knew who hadn't cared about white people was Muazena.

When white people came to their town, she preferred to lock herself in her hut and stay there until they were gone.

"If that's how it is, then of course you should go to

school," Lydia said. "But we'll have to mend your clothes. I don't want my daughters to be dressed worse than anyone else."

Maria and Sofia leaned forwards and clasped their hands around Lydia's strong arms in their joy. As soon as Lydia went inside to prepare for the night, they ran behind the hut, grasped each other's hands, and started dancing to a drumbeat they heard in the distance.

It was dark and they could barely see each other.

But you don't need to see happiness to understand it, or to be able to share it with someone else.

The same goes for sorrow and pain.

One thing the sisters knew was that there was nothing they liked so much as dancing. And the best dance of all was the dance of joy. No one had ever taught them to dance—it was something they had always known how to do. Sofia thought it must have begun when she was too little to walk, and had been tied to Mama Lydia's back. When Lydia danced with the other women, her movements and rhythms were transferred into Sofia's own body. They had been there ever since. It was the same for Maria.

They danced until Lydia came out and called for them to go to bed.

Later, when Lydia and Alfredo had fallen asleep, they lay awake whispering to each other.

"What if we're too stupid?" Maria said. "All we've ever done is hoe the fields."

"I don't think we're any stupider than anyone else," Sofia said. She tried to sound convincing, but deep down she was worried, too.

Early the following morning, before they went out to the fields to work, they sat with Lydia and mended their clothes. Lydia shook her head in despair.

"It won't get any better," she said. "I'll have to weave more baskets and sell them. You need new clothes, both of you."

The next day, Maria and Sofia went to school. They held each other by the hand and their steps got slower and slower the closer they came.

The school was a long, narrow building made of concrete, with lizards running around in the corners. There were no windows, just a sheet-metal roof held up by wooden poles. Lino came running when he noticed they had stopped on the road and obviously weren't going to come any closer.

"You have to speak to José-Maria," he said.

"Who's that?" Sofia asked.

"The priest," Lino answered with surprise. "And you have to talk to Filomena. The teacher."

He followed them to a corner of the school building where there was a small office.

"What do we do now?" Sofia asked.

"Don't you know anything?" Lino asked. "You knock on the door and go inside when someone calls."

Then he ran away. The boys were playing soccer with a ball made of tightly twisted and knotted straw.

"We're going home," said Maria.

"That's the last thing we're doing," Sofia answered. Then she knocked on the door. There was no reply. She knocked again. This time the door opened. The same white man who had looked at them with his sad smile when they first arrived was standing in the doorway. His face was sweaty and he'd put his glasses on his forehead.

"We want to start school," Sofia said.

The white man shuffled his glasses back on his nose.

"I remember you," he said. "Remarkable how you are so alike. Are you twins?"

"I'm Sofia," said Sofia. "This is Maria. There's a year between us. Maria is the oldest."

"What's your surname?"

"It's Alface." The name meant "salad" in their language.

The white man looked at them in amazement. Then he burst out laughing.

"That's a good name," he said. "Sofia and Maria Alface. Have you been to school before?"

They shook their heads.

"Then you should go to Filomena's class. I'll follow you there."

They went to the furthest classroom. The class had just begun. Filomena was young. And she was black.

"Two more students," José-Maria said. "Sofia and Maria. How many have you got now?"

"The last time I counted there were ninety-two students," Filomena said. "It'll work if they sit four to a bench."

José-Maria shook his head.

"We need to build a larger school," he said. "But where will we get the money?"

Then he left. Sofia and Maria stood with downcast eyes. All of the children in the classroom stared at them. They all seem so much younger than us, thought Sofia.

"Are you twins?" Filomena asked and smiled at them.

Sofia shook her head. Her mouth was so dry that she couldn't say a word.

Filomena pointed towards a bench where two girls were sitting.

"You can sit there," she said. "We have no books, no paper, and no pens. We don't even have chalk for the blackboard. Therefore, you'll have to remember everything. Sit down now."

And so they started school.

That night, after they'd gone to bed, Sofia couldn't sleep. She sneaked out of the hut and blew into the glowing coals of their fire until the flames returned.

She could hear drums from somewhere. Invisible grasshoppers creaked around her.

Looking deep into the fire, she thought she could see Muazena's face in the flames. And Hapakatanda's. They smiled at her.

She sat and stared into the fire and didn't know whether she wanted to laugh or cry. Maybe it was possible to do both at the same time. A crylaughter?

The flames of the fire danced in the night.

Sofia believed that the days ahead of her—the ones Muazena had compared to corn plants—would be bright. There were things other than monsters to be found hiding in the darkness.

There was a lot more to life.

And she was looking forward to it.

CHAPTER FOUR

A COUPLE OF DAYS after Maria and Sofia started school, José-Maria came and told them that everyone who had recently moved to the village was to meet that evening. The girls were to tell Lydia that everyone had to attend.

Maria was frightened.

"We might not be allowed to stay here," she said in a shaky voice.

"Why shouldn't we be able to?" Sofia answered. "Why would they let us start school if we're not supposed to stay?"

They were walking on the road home from school.

"Maybe there are bandits here, too?" said Maria. "Maybe we should all be leaving?"

Sometimes Sofia thought Maria had altogether too many questions. Why should she, who was younger, have to answer everything?

"I don't know," she said. "Don't ask me anything else right now."

In the evening, during the brief twilight when the sun set over the river, the people of the village met by the well in the middle of town.

José-Maria got up on a box so everyone could see him.

Then he told them about the landmines.

"When you go out to the fields, or down to the river, you must stick strictly to the well-trodden paths," he said. "It is safe to walk on them. But don't take any shortcuts. There are landmines. We don't know where they are. We only know that they are there."

"What's a landmine?" Maria asked her sister.

Sofia shushed her.

"I don't know," she said. "Don't talk so much. Listen instead."

"Landmines are bombs buried in the ground," José-Maria continued. "You can't see them. But if you put your foot on the ground above one, the mine will explode. You can have your leg blown off. You can be blinded. You can even die. Use only the paths. Never take shortcuts, not even if you're in a hurry."

Then he asked whether they had understood. Everyone nodded. They should stick to the paths. They were never to take shortcuts, not even if they were in a hurry.

On the way home, Lydia continued to lecture them. Sofia imagined the mines were like monsters buried in the ground, monsters that lay there waiting and spying.

Then she imagined them as crocodiles. Ground-crocodiles that waited to sink their teeth into her legs.

Lydia lectured them. Then Maria lectured Sofia. And Sofia lectured Alfredo.

Always the paths. Never shortcuts.

That evening, after they'd eaten their maize porridge, Sofia saw there was a full moon. She could recall that there had been a full moon when they arrived in the village. They'd been there for a month already.

She didn't exactly know what a month was. It was longer than a day and longer than a week, but it was less than a year. She didn't know how many full moons it had been since they fled the village where Hapakatanda and Muazena and all the dogs lay dead. Time was strange. It both existed and didn't exist.

The days were long. Maria and Sofia usually fell asleep right after they had eaten their evening meal and helped Lydia clean up. They got up at sunrise. By that time, Lydia had already left for the fields. They dressed Alfredo, and gave him some of the leftovers from the previous night's dinner. Then Sofia swept inside and outside the hut, while Maria took Alfredo to a woman who lived in a hut on the other side of the village. She was too old to work, but she looked after Alfredo until Lydia came back in the afternoon. When Maria had left Alfredo, they hurried over to the fields. They worked there until the sun was directly overhead, hoeing and weeding. They ate the food that Lydia and the other women prepared, then hurried down to the river to wash before running again so as not to be late for school. They were always careful to stay on the paths and they ran as fast as they could. But no matter how fast they ran neither of them ever got there before the other. Sofia could run faster, but Maria had more stamina.

Sometimes, despite the long days, they would have enough energy to stay awake and whisper to each other when Lydia and Alfredo had gone to sleep.

One night, as they lay with their faces close together, Maria asked if Sofia could remember her white dress.

Sophia remembered it well. The white dress their father Hapakatanda had once brought home from the town near their old village. He had only been able to afford one dress. But he'd promised that Sofia would also get one the next time he had money or something he could swap for it.

The dress had been left behind in the village on the night the bandits came.

"I sometimes dream that I'll wake up one morning and see that the dress is still here," Maria whispered.

"It probably got burned up," Sofia answered. "But one day, when I get some money, I'll buy you a new one."

"Where would you get money," Maria asked, "when Lydia hasn't got any? Don't forget, we're poor."

"I'll find a way," Sofia said.

"No, you won't," said Maria.

"I promise," said Sofia.

After Maria had fallen asleep, Sofia lay pondering what Maria had said. How was she to get a new white dress for Maria? She'd promised, and Maria would never forget her promise. She knew that somehow or other she would have to keep it.

She knew that she made promises to Maria far too easily. It had happened many times before, and it upset her.

Time passed—time that both existed and didn't exist. There was another full moon. Every day it got hotter and hotter. There was less and less water in the river. But the rains would soon be coming.

One day, when they had a holiday from school and Maria was lying in the hut with pains in her stomach, Sofia went out to explore. The huts were spread across a large area, and until now she had only seen a small part of the village.

When she reached the other side, Sofia came across a man sitting outside a hut sewing clothes. He was treadling a black sewing machine. Sofia had seen a sewing machine once before. There had been an Indian who, for a short time, had tried to make a living from making clothes in her old village. He had sat in the shade of a tree and treadled his strange machine. All the children in town used to stand around him watching with fascination. Sofia hadn't been more than five or six at the time, but she could still remember the sewing machine. She'd thought then that she'd like to learn how to use a machine like that when she grew up.

Before long, the Indian had left the village and taken his machine with him. The people in town were far too poor to be able to pay him to make clothes.

Sofia could still remember how sad she had been when he left town. The sewing machine had been tied to his back.

Now she saw a sewing machine again.

It looked like the one the Indian had owned.

She stood there, watching the man treadling and sewing.

When he looked up from his work and noticed her, she looked down and thought she had better leave.

But the man smiled and nodded. Carefully, she ventured a little closer.

His name was Antonio but people called him Totio. He was old and had no teeth. His wife Fernanda was inside the hut. Their children were grown up and had their own families. Totio and Fernanda had run away from the bandits, too. They had abandoned everything except for the sewing machine.

He told Sofia all of this while he treadled the machine and kept sewing. He was making a pair of black trousers.

Fernanda came out of the hut and sat on a straw mat in the shade. She was fat, and breathed heavily in the heat.

"Who are you?" she called to Sofia from the mat. "If you've got money, Totio will sew you anything. If you've got a lot of money he can sew you a pair of wings."

"She's only talking," Totio said and laughed. "I can't sew wings."

He winked at her and wiped the sweat from his forehead.

"Have you got a name?" he asked.

"My name is Sofia."

He continued to ask her about who she was and where she came from, sewing the whole time. Sofia answered as well as she could. From time to time Fernanda shouted from the straw mat. Then she fell asleep and started snoring.

"I have a good wife," Totio said. "Sometimes she talks too much. But she's a good wife."

"I'd like to learn how to sew," Sofia said.

Totio laughed.

"I bet you would," he said.

The trousers were finished. He checked them and hung them carefully on the edge of the table.

Then he patted the sewing machine.

"Good job, Xio."

Sofia looked at him with surprise.

"Why shouldn't a sewing machine have a name?" Totio said. "And why do you want to learn how to sew?"

"I want to make a white dress for my sister Maria," she said. She hadn't worked out the answer beforehand. It just came out on its own.

Then she thought she should explain why she wanted to sew that particular dress. She told Totio about what happened the night Hapakatanda died and about him coming home from the city with the dress for Maria.

When she had explained everything, Totio nodded thoughtfully.

"It's like that," he said. "They kill and burn and plunder. But no one considers the fact that the bandits also stole a white dress from a girl called Maria."

"I promised her the dress," Sofia said.

"Bring me the fabric and I'll teach you how to sew," said Totio. "If you can get a nice piece of cloth and the right thread, I'll teach you how to do it. First by hand and then, if you're clever, you'll learn how to use the machine."

Sofia couldn't believe her ears. Was she really going to be allowed to treadle the machine?

But how was she going to get a piece of fabric?

At that moment Fernanda woke up.

"Go now," said Totio. "I don't have time to talk to you anymore. Come back and see me when you have the fabric and the thread."

Sofia walked home. But first she followed one of the winding paths down to the river. There was a mound there where she and Maria would sit and watch for crocodiles. It was far enough from the water for there to be no danger of a crocodile getting them. But on this particular day Sofia wasn't concerned about the crocodiles. How was she going to get a piece of fabric for Maria's dress? She didn't have any money, and Mama Lydia didn't have any either.

Then she remembered the clean, white sheets that were usually hung out to dry outside José-Maria's house. Maybe she could ask for one of them? But she dismissed that idea right away. She would never dare. Besides, José-Maria would probably be angry with her for begging. He might even chase her family from the village.

Sofia stayed by the river for so long that it was already dusk when she got up and went home. When she reached the hut, she could tell Lydia was angry.

"Where have you been all day?" she asked loudly.

Sofia looked down when she answered.

"Nowhere," she said.

"Nowhere?" said Lydia. "I thought you'd fallen into the river. Or gotten lost. Why can't you stay at home when your sister is ill?"

"I'm feeling fine now, Mama," Maria called from inside the hut.

"Go and fetch water," Lydia said. "Hurry up. It's getting dark."

That night Sofia had difficulties falling asleep. She thought of Totio. She thought about the white fabric that she would never be able to get hold of. And about the promise she'd made Maria.

But most of all she thought about the white sheets.

They were often hanging there at dawn, which meant they had been there all night.

José-Maria had many sheets. He probably wouldn't notice if one of them went missing. José-Maria surely didn't keep count of his sheets. He had so much else to think about.

Sofia opened her eyes in the darkness.

What was she thinking of? Stealing a sheet? Was she going to make a dress out of stolen cloth?

Did she want Maria to wear clothes that a thief had taken?

She huddled up in the darkness. Her thoughts frightened her.

I can't steal one of José-Maria's sheets, she thought. There has to be another way.

But Sofia didn't find any other way. And in the mornings that followed, when she and Maria walked out to the fields, she could see the white sheets waving in the light morning breeze outside José-Maria's house.

There was yet another cycle of the moon. When it was full again, Sofia knew she couldn't wait any longer. One night, when everyone was asleep, she carefully got up, pushed aside the straw mat that hung in front of the doorway, and slipped into the darkness. She held her breath and listened. Everything was quiet. Somewhere a rat rustled. A child moaned in its sleep inside a hut.

Then her fear came crawling.

What would happen if somebody saw her?

I'll go back to bed, she thought. I can't do it. Even if I just borrow the sheet, it will still be José-Maria's, even when it's a dress for Maria.

At the same time, she knew her promise to Maria was more important. She ran through the darkness, past the dark huts, past the still-smouldering coals of many fires.

The sheets were hanging there. They were like

white, restless spirits in the moonlight. She stood still and listened.

I don't dare, she thought. I don't dare.

Then she crept swiftly across to the clothesline, plucked off a sheet, pulled two others together so there wouldn't be a gap, and ran away.

Suddenly it felt as if every person in the village was awake. She imagined they were watching through cracks in the hut walls. They could see her—Sofia, Lydia's daughter, Maria's sister—the thief who had stolen one of José-Maria's sheets.

She didn't stop running until she was back at the hut, where she had to bend over to get her breath back.

There was a hole in a tree that grew close to the old brick and iron fireplace. She stuffed the sheet into the hole and covered it up with soil.

Then she carefully drew aside the straw mat and went back to bed.

"What are you doing?" Maria said suddenly.

Sofia thought her heart would stop. Had Maria been awake the whole time she'd been away?

"I just had to go to the toilet," she replied.

But Maria was already asleep.

Sofia lay awake until dawn. Several times she was on the verge of running with the sheet to hang it back on the line. But when dawn came and Lydia left the hut, the sheet was still in the tree. She waited until

Lydia had gone, then hurried outside before Maria woke and wrapped the sheet around her body under the *capulana* she usually wore.

A few weeks later they had school holidays. José-Maria hadn't complained that he was missing any sheets. Sofia was always frightened when she met him. She had a guilty conscience and was sorry she'd stolen it.

It will always be his sheet, she said to herself. Even when Maria is wearing it as a dress.

When she went to Totio with the sheet she was afraid he might ask where she'd got hold of it. But he said nothing, just looked at it and nodded.

"I don't have any thread," Sofia said.

"I'll give you some," said Totio. "After all, the fabric was the main thing."

That week, with Totio's help, Sofia sewed a dress for Maria. She was never allowed to treadle the machine, but Totio said she would certainly learn how.

"I've spoken to Xio," said Totio, nodding towards the sewing machine. "He believes you and he will become friends one day."

"So the sewing machine is a he?" Sofia asked.

"I think so," Totio answered with surprise. It seemed it had never occurred to him that the sewing machine could be a she.

"At least, he's never protested against his name," he said. "And Xio is no name for a woman."

When Maria wanted to know what Sofia was doing in the afternoons, Sofia just said it was a secret.

"It's something for you," she said. "Don't ask any more questions."

The dress was ready. It was beautiful. Sofia could hardly wait for Maria to wear it.

But there was a problem. How was she going to explain where she got it? How was she going to make Lydia believe she was telling the truth?

As she stood there with the dress in her hand, she thought she had better ask for Totio's help.

"Mama Lydia might ask where I got the fabric," she said. "I found a banknote on the ground. Instead of giving it to her, I bought the fabric. She might be angry with me."

Totio laughed. It saddened Sofia to know how easy it was to lie.

"I can say you got it from me," he said. "Don't worry about it."

That evening, Sofia gave Maria the dress. She didn't want Lydia to see it. Not until Maria had put it on. She gave it to Maria on the little hill down by the river.

Maria couldn't believe her eyes. It fit perfectly.

Sofia had used her own measurements and then just made the dress slightly bigger.

"I made it myself," Sofa said. "That was the secret. And I got the fabric from an old man who has a sewing machine. His name is Totio. Do you remember the Indian who sat under the tree and sewed on a machine? Totio has one exactly like that."

Sofia saw how happy Maria was. Maria wanted to run home at once to show it to Lydia.

"Wait until tomorrow," Sofia said. "It's Sunday. It'll be a surprise for her, too."

Lydia was just as surprised as Maria. To Sofia's relief, she believed the explanation. The following day, she went over to Totio and thanked him for showing Sofia how to sew.

Sofia dreaded her return. But Lydia just smiled.

"Totio said you were clever," she said.

"I'd very much like to learn to sew," said Sofia.

Sofia thought less and less often about the fact that the dress was actually José-Maria's sheet. Maria wanted to wear the dress all the time, even when she was out in the fields. She would just hitch it up and wrap her *capulana* over it.

A few more full moons came and went.

Every morning, Sofia and Maria ran out to the

women in the fields. It would soon be harvest time. The plants were already tall.

They played as they ran. They leaped in unison, or tried to avoid touching the stones that stuck out of the ground. They always made a game of it.

One morning, when it had been raining overnight and the red dirt on the path was still wet, Sofia had the idea that they should take turns closing their eyes while they ran. She gave it a try to see if it worked, and ran a little ways with her eyes shut. Maria was just behind her.

It wasn't hard. She would try again. One last time. Then she would let Maria play the game as well.

It may have been because the ground was wet, but she stumbled and took a couple of strides off the path. Maria was alongside her. Sofia opened her eyes and saw she was off the path. The game was probably more difficult than she'd imagined.

"What are you doing?" said Maria, who was still standing on the path.

"Nothing," said Sofia. "I'm playing."

She hopped on her left foot.

Then she put her right foot down to take a step back onto the path.

And then the ground exploded.

CHAPTER FIVE

AFTERWARDS, everything was silent. Sofia thought she was lying in an ants' nest, with thousands of angry ants biting and tearing at her body. It was as if she had ants inside her stomach, in her head, and in her legs as well. She was lying on her side. She had difficulty seeing clearly and the pain was so bad that she couldn't even cry.

Maria was a few steps away, lying face down, halfway into a bush. Sofia noticed that her white dress was gone, the one she'd been so fond of. Now there were just a few rags hanging around her waist. And they were no longer white, either. They were red. Sofia realized it was blood.

She tried to scream again, to call out to Maria, to Mama Lydia. She felt as though she were falling: the ants bit and tore at her body, and then she sank into a bottomless darkness.

José-Maria was standing with a cup of coffee in his hand and was about to lift it to his lips when he heard the explosion. He knew at once what had happened. Someone had stepped on a landmine. His face twisted with fear. He didn't even give himself time to put the cup on a table, and threw it aside. Then he flung open the door and ran in the direction of the blast: some-where down by the river, by the outer fields. As he ran he shouted at people to fetch the nun called Rut, who was a nurse. He ran as fast as he could. It was already hot, although it wasn't more than six o'clock in the morning. His heart pumped wildly in his chest, and he dreaded what he might see.

He wasn't the first to arrive. Women had come running from the fields and he could hear them screaming.

It's one of them, he thought. But why did she leave the path? They know there are landmines.

He noticed he was almost angry.

When he arrived, several of the women grabbed him and tried to explain what had happened, but he couldn't understand what they were saying. He forced his way through and stopped short.

What he saw made him weep. It was the two girls who looked so alike, Sofia and Maria. He bent over the one who lay in the middle of the path. He thought it was Sofia but wasn't sure. He dropped to his knees and flung his arms out.

It was a bloody lump that lay in front of him. It

barely resembled a person any longer—it was just blood, shattered limbs, and ragged clothes.

But she was still breathing. He yelled at the women to be quiet and told them to find the girls' mother. By now some men had arrived as well.

"Where's Sister Rut?" he shouted. "Take off your shirts, find some branches, and sling the shirts in between so we can use them as stretchers."

Then he crawled on his knees across to the other girl who was lying face down. He tried to feel her pulse.

She's dead, he thought. Oh my God, I can't bear this.

Then he felt her pulse. It was very weak.

He heard Sister Rut's voice as she came running.

"They're alive!" José-Maria shouted.

He stood up on shaking legs while Rut, in turn, bent over the two girls. She'd brought a bag with her, and quickly started bandaging Sofia, and then Maria. One of the women helped her.

A man touched José-Maria's shoulder and pointed.

The girls' mother was running towards them. She hadn't seen anything, but she was screaming— screaming so loudly that it cut through him.

"What's her name?" he asked. "Has she got a husband?"

"Lydia," replied one of the men. "Her husband was killed by the bandits."

"She shouldn't see this," José-Maria said.

He tried to intercept Lydia as she ran closer, but she fought herself free. It was only when the other men grabbed her as well that she was held back.

But by then it was too late.

She had already seen her daughters lying on the path.

She stopped screaming.

Then an unearthly howl burst from her.

José-Maria would never forget it.

Her howl would haunt him for the rest of his life.

The stretchers were ready and Rut had done all she could. Carefully they started to shift Maria. All they could hear was a weak moan. Someone lightly laid a *capulana* over her and they carried her up towards the road where a truck stood waiting.

Then they lifted Sofia onto the other stretcher.

As they lifted her up, her left foot came loose and remained lying on the path. Rut picked it up carefully and placed it on the stretcher. José-Maria turned away and vomited.

When they arrived at the hospital in the city, José-Maria thought it was already too late.

"They're dead," he said.

Sister Rut shook her head.

"They're alive. They're still breathing."

"Are they going to be all right?" José-Maria asked.

"We'll have to have faith that they will," Rut replied.

José-Maria nodded. He thought about the girls' mother, Lydia, who had been left behind with the other women.

He felt a mixture of despair and rage such as he'd never felt before.

He was a priest. He believed in God. He believed in a God who had created the world and the animals and the humans, the ocean and the sun, the moon and the stars. A God who was good.

How, then, could this be possible? Two poverty-stricken children, torn to pieces, lying on a path one early morning.

Rut seemed to read his mind. She took his hand and shook her head.

Sofia and Maria were transferred to two other stretchers. The hospital was poor, José-Maria knew that. It lacked almost everything. On many of the hospital beds there weren't even sheets. But the nurses and doctors were capable.

One of the nurses was called Celeste, another one Marta. They'd seen plenty of landmine victims.

But now they looked at Sofia and Maria.

"I know you shouldn't think like this," Marta said, "but wouldn't it have been better if these children had died?"

"They no doubt will," Celeste replied. "They'll never survive these injuries."

At that moment a doctor walked in. His name was Raul. He hadn't heard what the two nurses had been saying. He was young, and felt the same helpless rage as José-Maria when he saw what landmines did to people.

He examined Sofia and then Maria.

Although Maria had fewer wounds, he knew at once that her injuries were worse. The blast from the explosion had damaged her internally. She was bleeding from the inside, unlike the other girl, who had lost her foot and had her legs and her belly torn apart.

The girls were wheeled away so he could begin operating. He turned to José-Maria, who was still there. Rut had already gone back to take care of the girls' mother.

"What happened?" Doctor Raul asked.

José-Maria flung his arms out.

"They knew they weren't supposed to leave the path," he said. "Yet it happens, all the same."

"It will happen as long as there are landmines," Doctor Raul answered. He made no attempt to hide his anger.

"Are they going to survive?" José-Maria asked.

Doctor Raul had to think before he replied.

"I don't know," he said. "Most likely not."

"Neither of them?"

"Maybe the one that lost her foot. The other girl has severe internal injuries."

Doctor Raul operated for many hours, along with several other doctors.

In the end, tired and sweaty, they knew there was only one thing they could do.

Wait.

Maria and Sofia lay in two beds set close to each other. There was complete silence in the room. A nurse sat on a chair by the window. It was dawn again: the sun was rising above the horizon and the roofs of the city.

Two doctors came into the room.

Sofia was asleep. But she was aware of what was happening around her. She heard two men talking. Had her papa come? No, he was dead. It had to be someone else. Or perhaps she had dreamed it all? There hadn't been any monsters that night.

She didn't know. In her sleep she could hear the two men talking to each other. They spoke with low voices.

"Maria is probably not going to make it," said one of the voices. "The injuries are too severe. We can't stop the infections."

"She's strong," said the other voice. "They're both strong."

"We'll have to wait. That's all we can do."

The voices stopped and the footsteps moved away. Deep in the darkness, Sofia tried to comprehend what she'd heard. But then surging pains made her drift away on a dark, underground ocean.

It felt as though fires were burning inside her. Why was she in so much pain? The last thing she remembered was that she and Maria had been on their way out to the fields to work. Maria had been wearing her white dress. Sofia had been angry with her because she would get it dirty out there in the fields. They'd been running and pushing each other, she remembered. Pushing each other and laughing and running. Then everything was gone.

She was drifting on the dark ocean and the fires kept burning inside her.

Suddenly she thought she heard Maria calling. But she couldn't see her. She listened while she drifted. Now she could hear it clearly: Maria was calling her.

She came to the surface with a jerk. The fires kept burning. It was agonizing. But she opened her eyes. She didn't know where she was. The room was strange to her. It wasn't their hut. Cold, tall, white walls. From a doorway, a dim light shone into the room. When she turned her head—carefully, since every one of her movements hurt—she could see a woman dressed in white sitting on a chair by the window, with her chin on her chest. It was a nurse; Sofia could tell, because she had a white hat on her head. She was sleeping. Sofia turned her head again. Next to her bed there was another bed and Maria was lying in it. The light from the door shone on her pale face.

Suddenly Maria opened her eyes and looked at Sofia.

"I want to go home, Sofia," she said. "I'm in so much pain."

Sofia reached out, although the pain shot straight through her. But she had to do it. If she didn't, Maria would get out of the bed and leave. She would be left on her own. Apart from the sleeping woman by the window, she would be the only person left on earth.

Her hand reached Maria. Sofia caught hold of her sister.

"I'm in so much pain," Maria said. "I want to go home."

"It's nighttime," Sofia said. "We'll go home tomorrow."

Maria sat up in bed.

"I'm going home now," she said.

Then she lay down. She looked at Sofia.

Then she closed her eyes.

Sofia knew that Maria had died. Her hand twitched. Then she was gone.

Sofia screamed.

The woman by the window woke and stood up. She turned on the light and looked at Sofia. Then she looked at Maria.

She tried to remove Sofia's hand. But Sofia would not let go.

Then Sofia sank into the darkness again. Maria was somewhere down there, she knew that.

It would soon be morning.

Then everything would be back to normal. They'd hurry out to the fields where Mama Lydia would already be squatting with her hoe.

Then it would be afternoon and they'd walk to school.

Everything would be as usual.

If only the fires inside her would stop burning.

She never noticed the white-clad people who walked into the room. She never saw Doctor Raul stand quietly by Maria's bed and shake his head.

She never saw them transferring Maria to a trolley and wheeling her from the room.

She never saw that they covered her with a clean, unused sheet.

Doctor Raul had brought the sheet with him from his own home. He hadn't wanted Maria to be covered by a sheet that was ripped and dirty.

The next time Sofia woke it was daytime. The sun was shining in through the window. She could hear cars outside.

Then she discovered that Maria was gone. Her bed was empty.

She vaguely remembered what had happened during the night.

Maria has gone home, she thought. She's left me here. All by myself. Why has she done that?

A nurse came into the room.

"Where's Maria?" Sofia asked.

"Maria's dead," the nurse said.

Sofia shook her head.

"She's gone home," Sofia said. "She's not dead."

At that moment Doctor Raul came in. Sofia didn't know his name. He looked kind, but his face was drawn with weariness.

"Where's Maria?" Sofia asked.

Doctor Raul crouched by her bed.

"Your sister was very tired," he said. "She had such terrible injuries that all she wanted to do was to sleep. That's what she's doing right now. She's no longer in pain. I think we should be happy about that, even though we're sad that she's gone. She was in so much pain, Sofia. That's why Maria is dead."

Sofia looked into his eyes.

He stroked her forehead gently.

"Your Mama Lydia is out there," he said. "I'll go and get her."

Doctor Raul left the room and closed the door. Outside, in the corridor, Lydia sat hunched on the floor in despair. José-Maria stood next to her.

Doctor Raul squatted in front of Lydia.

"You have to think about Sofia now," he said. "Go in to see her. But don't cry, don't scream. Remember that Sofia is very ill."

Lydia nodded. José-Maria had to pull her up from the floor. Then he helped her into the room where Sofia lay.

They said almost nothing to each other. José-Maria stood at the back of the room. He watched how Lydia stroked Sofia with her hands, and how Sofia followed Lydia's face with her eyes.

Then Lydia left. Out in the corridor, she fainted.

Two days later the doctors removed Sofia's right leg from just above the knee. They couldn't save it. They still hoped she could keep the other leg, although it was also badly injured.

Four days later, Doctor Raul realized they wouldn't be able to save the other leg after all. The next day he removed it from just below the knee.

Sofia still wasn't aware that she no longer had legs.

The night after the second operation she was drifting on the underground ocean. The fires continued to burn inside her. Two nurses came into her room. She heard their footsteps, and noticed how they lifted the sheet and examined her body.

Then she heard them talking to each other.

"It would have been better for her to have died like her sister," said one of the voices.

"What kind of life is waiting for her in the future?" said the other.

Then the room went quiet. The footsteps moved away from her and the door closed.

Sofia opened her eyes.

Had they been talking about her? Why would it have been better if she had died too? Why wasn't Maria's death enough?

She noticed something strange about her body. It wasn't only the burning fires. She ran her hand carefully down her chest and belly, across all the bandages, and continued down one of her legs.

It stopped at her knee. Her leg was gone.

They've removed it, she thought fearfully.

They've taken one of my legs away from me.

CHAPTER SIX

SOFIA SAT LOOKING into the fire.

She was dreaming, but everything seemed so real that she could smell the burned wood, the grass, and the soil.

She didn't look for secrets in the fire this time. She looked for Muazena's face among the flames. She wanted to ask about the leg that had disappeared, the leg that someone had taken away from her.

But Muazena's face wasn't there. Sofia sat and stared into the fire until there was nothing but smouldering coals. And then darkness.

When she woke, there was a new day. The pains came and went in waves. Again she felt with her hand beneath the sheet. The leg was gone. At her knee there was only a stump, wrapped in bandages.

She was very tired. The pain throbbed. She was too tired to think about what had happened to her leg. It felt as if she'd been running a long way and needed to catch her breath. Maybe she'd run so fast that one of her legs got left behind? Maybe it would soon be back in its place below her knee?

Doctor Raul came into her room. She recognized him now, although she still didn't know his name. But he always sat by her bed so that his face was close to her own. He smiled. He looked tired. Wasn't there a bed where he could lie down and rest?

"How are you, Sofia?" he asked.

"Someone has taken one of my legs," she answered.

She spoke so softly that he barely heard what she was saying. He leaned closer and asked her to repeat it.

"One of my legs is gone," Sofia said.

He looked into her tired eyes. Her face was covered with cuts from the explosion. He felt the rage in his heart again. This is a child who has been deprived of the ability to run, he thought. An African girl who will never dance again.

Doctor Raul realized that she thought only one of her legs was gone. She still hadn't noticed that they had also removed the second one.

He knew he would have to tell her. That would be better than letting her find out for herself when she was alone.

He wished he didn't have to. He wished he would never again have to see a girl like Sofia in a hospital bed, torn to pieces by a landmine.

Even so, he dared to believe that this girl would survive. There was still a risk that she could get infections, but he thought she might make it. She had an unusual strength. Of course, he would never fully understand the torment she was enduring—but she was strong.

He'd heard from the nurses that Sofia rarely cried. She suffered silently through all the pain.

Strength had nothing to do with a man being able to lift a huge weight above his head.

Strength was a girl who survived treading on a landmine.

Doctor Raul leaned close to her.

"It's not only one of your legs that is gone," he said. "We had to remove the other one, too. If we hadn't, you would never have recovered. But I can promise that you'll get two fine artificial legs. And you'll be able to walk again, Sofia. I promise you that. You'll get two new legs. They'll be your best friends for the rest of your life."

He looked at her face.

"Do you understand what I'm telling you?" he asked.

Sofia didn't take her eyes off him. She explored her body with her hand. The other leg was gone, too. She looked at Doctor Raul.

"I want my legs back," she said.

"You'll get new legs," Doctor Raul answered.

"I don't want new ones," she said. "I want my old ones."

She hadn't the energy to say anything else. The pain was too great. A nurse gave her something to drink. She was soon asleep.

In Sofia's restless dreams, Maria was still alive. But the images were shattered and confusing. The white dress was hanging on José-Maria's clothesline. There were many white dresses hanging there, but no sheets. Totio was treadling his sewing machine. Lydia was crushing corn. Sofia kept looking for Maria the whole time. But she had always just disappeared, was always invisible. Sofia knew Maria was there, but she couldn't see her.

Sometimes when she woke up the pain was almost gone. If she lay totally still, without moving, it almost felt like normal.

It was at those moments, when the pain had ceased for a while, that she thought she should speak to José-Maria. She wanted to tell him that it was she who had taken the sheet. If she confessed, he would surely help her to get her old legs back.

He came to the hospital twice a week with Lydia. He usually came into her room on his own before fetching Lydia from the corridor.

Sofia told him the next time he visited.

At first he thought she was delirious. What was this sheet she was talking about? A white dress for Maria?

Then he understood that she had taken a sheet

from his clothesline. The sheet had become a dress for Maria, who was now dead.

José-Maria remembered seeing the bloody white rags on Maria's body as she lay face down on the path where the mine had exploded. But he had never noticed that a sheet had disappeared.

Sofia looked frightened. It was important that he took her seriously.

"It doesn't matter," he said. "You shouldn't think about that now."

"In that case, maybe I could get my legs back," Sofia said.

José-Maria was touched. This was a remarkable girl, lying there in bed, tiny and pale. Even black people can turn pale with pain and sorrow, he thought. "You'll get new legs," he said. "Your old legs couldn't manage any longer."

Then he went out to the corridor to fetch Lydia.

"She knows her legs are gone," he told her. "It's important that you remember she'll be getting new legs."

Lydia was sitting on the floor in the corridor. It was crowded with people.

"How is she going to manage?" she asked. "We're so poor."

"Let her recover first," José-Maria said. "Then we can start thinking about the future. Go in and see her now! Don't cry. Don't shout. Tell her the whole village is waiting for her to come home."

It was always difficult for Lydia to visit Sofia: to see her suffering face, to think that underneath the sheet her legs were gone. She felt so helpless. And what was her own life going to be like later on—having Sofia back in the village without legs? Sometimes she felt she'd lost everything in life. She had once been young, as young as Sofia. She had met Hapakatanda and they'd lived a good life together. Then the bandits had come out of the darkness and everything had changed. Ever since then they had been running away. And just when she finally felt she could start building a new life with her children, horror had struck again.

Would it never end? Would the rest of her life be nothing but worry and pain?

Sofia's spirits always lifted when Mama Lydia came. She didn't like being alone in her room. This visit, she hadn't the energy to say too much herself, but she listened to Lydia, who talked without a break. Lydia talked about Alfredo, and about the maize that was ready to be harvested. But she never mentioned Maria. Finally, when she ran out of things to say, the room fell silent. A lonely fly buzzed above Sofia's face. Lydia, who had been sitting on the floor beside the bed, got up and stroked her lightly on one of her cheeks.

"I'll come back soon," she said.

Sofia nodded. When she moved her head the pain

returned. She had to will herself not to start scream-ing. She didn't want Lydia to hear.

The same night, as Sofia lay alone in her room drifting on the underground waves, and as Lydia slept huddled with Alfredo on the floor of the hut, José-Maria sat on the bed in his room holding a small crucifix. A single lamp lit the room.

José-Maria was a priest. He believed in God. Long ago, when he was growing up in Brazil, he had decided to be ordained. Some years later he'd been sent as a missionary to Africa, to a country where there was a civil war and many people were suffering.

Several years had passed since then. José-Maria sometimes thought that he had problems with his God. He had difficulties coming to terms with what happened to people.

Or was it the other way around? Was it God that had a problem with José-Maria?

He often sat with the crucifix at night, trying to talk to God.

This particular night he was talking about Sofia. He tried to understand why anyone should have to suffer as she had. And why did her sister have to die?

He thought he could hear a tired voice inside him-self. It was as if he himself were talking, but as a very old man. The voice was old and rusty, the words vague as forgotten whispers.

God is a mystery, he thought. The silence I meet is God's own despair.

José-Maria sat with his crucifix in his hand far into the night.

Then he turned off the lamp.

Some weeks passed. Sofia drifted on the underground waves less and less often. The pains grew weaker. She was sometimes hungry and started sitting up in bed to eat. One day, when she was alone, she pulled the sheet away and saw with her own eyes that her legs were gone. The stumps were wrapped in big bandages.

There was something peculiar about the parts of the legs that were gone. She could still feel them, all the way down to her feet.

They're calling me, she thought.

They're just as lonely as I am.

The same day she asked Doctor Raul what had happened to her legs.

Her question surprised him. However, one thing he had learned about Sofia was that it was best to tell the truth.

"Your legs are dead," he said. "They were dead but you're alive. We burned them. Then we buried them."

Sofia thought about what he'd said for a long time.

"I hope you buried them next to Maria," she said.

Doctor Raul nodded slowly.

"Yes," he said. "We did bury them next to Maria."

The next day, Sofia was allowed up for the first time. How long she'd been lying in her bed, she didn't know. She hoped it had been a long time. The more time that passed since Maria's death, the easier it became to think about her. One of the nurses lifted Sofia into a rusty old wheelchair with crooked wheels. Then she pushed Sofia out through the door. The corridor was full of sick people. It smelled of sweat and wounds.

"You need some fresh air," said the nurse, whose name was Mariza.

They came out onto the pavement outside the hospital. Sofia looked with surprise at the cars passing on the street, the tall buildings, and all the people hurrying by. Mariza put the wheelchair close to the hospital wall.

"You can sit here and watch," she said smiling. "I'll come and fetch you later."

She wrapped a dirty blanket around Sofia's legs. Sofia hoped no one would be able to see that she didn't have legs anymore.

Then she was alone.

She had no memories of coming to the city. The last thing she remembered was that she and Maria had been running along the path leading to the fields.

She suddenly realized she had absolutely no idea

what had happened. Why was Maria dead? Why didn't she have her legs anymore? Why hadn't anyone told her what had happened?

Had the bandits returned?

Her thoughts wandered back and forth while she sat in the wheelchair outside the hospital. All around her, women were sitting on the pavement with various goods spread in front of them. Some had made small tables from cardboard boxes. They were selling oranges and apples, onions and peas, pieces of chocolate and maize. Some also had cans of beer. Every now and then, a person would stop and buy something. The women chatted to each other the whole time, breast-feeding their children and arranging their goods.

Suddenly Sofia noticed someone talking to her in her own language. It was a woman who was sitting quite close by. She offered Sofia half an orange. Sofia shook her head; she didn't have any money to pay for it. Then she recognized that she was being given the orange. She accepted it.

"What happened to you?" asked the woman. She was young and had a brilliant smile.

"I don't know," Sofia answered. "Something happened to my legs. And Maria died."

"Was that your mother?"

"My sister."

"*Yo Mammanû, inû,*" the woman wailed. "The war kills everyone. What's your name?"

"Sofia Alface."

"My name is Miranda," the woman said. "I'll be your friend."

The orange tasted better than anything Sofia had ever eaten. She looked at the woman and suddenly she couldn't help laughing.

But it sounded strange.

She had almost forgotten how to laugh.

The following week, Mariza wheeled Sofia outside once each morning and again in the afternoons. Miranda was there every day. Sometimes Doctor Raul came out onto the street to smoke a cigarette. Once he gave Miranda some banknotes.

Miranda kept giving Sofia oranges, and Sofia soon figured out that Doctor Raul was paying for them.

Sofia soon knew all the women who surrounded her on the street. The called out when Mariza came with the wheelchair and sometimes, when they had errands to run, they let Sofia sit with some of the smallest children in her lap. She was usually sitting outside on the street when Mama Lydia and José-Maria came to visit.

One day, Mariza came to fetch her earlier than usual.

"You're going to meet Master Emilio," she said.

"Who is that?" Sofia asked.

"He's the one who will be making your new legs," Mariza said.

Master Emilio was in a room full of arms and legs and feet and hands. Sofia thought the room was creepy at first. But Master Emilio laughed as he shook her hand, reminding her of Totio, and he said that everything would be all right. He was going to make a couple of really nice legs for Sofia. He would make them out of plastic and she'd get black shoes.

Then, with some help from Mariza, he carefully removed her bandages. Sofia saw the wounds on her knees for the first time. They still hadn't healed. She felt sick and looked away. Master Emilio was busy with a tape measure, writing down numbers in a note-book. Then the two of them replaced the bandages.

"You'll have to practise walking again," said Master Emilio. "It's going to be difficult. But you'll succeed."

Sofia nodded.

"You do want to learn how to walk again?" he asked.

"Yes," Sofia said.

But deep inside she didn't know what she wanted. There were days and nights when she thought only about Maria: Maria who was dead and who would never again exist. Even if she got a couple of artificial legs, she would never be able to run again, never be able to dance. She would have to use crutches.

Maybe it would have been better if she had died, too. Her legs were already waiting for her under the ground.

She didn't tell anyone about her thoughts. Not Mama Lydia, not José-Maria, not Doctor Raul.

Early one morning, Doctor Raul came into her room.

"You're going to move today," he said. "We need this room for other people who are more ill than you."

As usual, he had squatted down next to her bed.

"You'll be fine," he said. "No one can make such nice legs as Master Emilio. It's time for you to learn how to walk again."

"Am I going home?" Sofia asked.

Doctor Raul shook his head.

"That's too far away," he answered. "You have to stay here in the city for a while yet, until your legs are ready and you can walk properly. It's too far a drive to pick you up every day."

Mariza came to get Sofia late in the afternoon. She wheeled her outside in the rusty chair to where a car stood waiting, then helped her into the car.

"I'll see you tomorrow," Mariza said.

The car rushed through the city. Sofia was scared. She had no idea where she was going. What if she just disappeared among all the people, she and her wheel-chair? No one would ever find her.

She tried to take notice of the route they took. But the myriad of streets just confused her. In the end, she couldn't even work out in which direction the hospital lay.

The car finally turned in through the gates of a big compound containing several large buildings. The car stopped and the driver lifted out Sofia and the wheelchair.

"This is where you're going to live," he said. "It's an old people's home. Every morning a car will come and take you to the hospital. That's where you'll learn how to walk."

Then the car drove off. Sofia sat in her wheel-chair. In her lap she had an orange that Miranda had given her.

She looked around.

There were no people to be seen.

She was alone. The sun was about to set.

It would soon be night.

She had been abandoned.

CHAPTER SEVEN

SOFIA SAT IN her wheelchair all night. The stars shone and twinkled above her. From time to time she slept. She had pulled the blanket over her head and every time she woke from her restless sleep she wondered where she was.

Forgotten, she thought. Rejected. They needed my bed at the hospital. Lydia will never find me again. The wheelchair will sink into the ground.

Sofia wasn't afraid of the dark. But she was scared because she couldn't move. When darkness fell she had tried to wheel the chair, but the wheels were so crooked that they were impossible to move. For as long as she could, she kept trusting that someone would come. But once it was dark and the many sounds of the city gradually died away, she realized she was going to stay there the whole night.

She thought she might be able to lift herself out of the chair and crawl across to one of the trees that grew close to the building. But she stayed where she was. Her leg stumps itched underneath the bandages.

She sang throughout the night to keep herself company. If she sang really loud, Maria might be able to hear her from where she was under the ground. She sang all the songs she could remember. She sang loud and long, fast and slow, again and again. It reduced her fear of being alone. It also helped her to avoid thinking about what would happen when the night was over.

She remembered how things had been when she was young. Hapakatanda had sometimes shown her and Maria the stars at night. He'd shown them how you could see formations that looked like animals. He'd also told them that everyone should choose their own star.

"There is a star for every person," he said. "It will shine for as long as that person lives. When they die and go to live with their ancestors, the star shoots off and disappears."

Sofia also remembered that she had asked if you buried shooting stars. Her question had surprised Hapakatanda.

"I never thought about that," he said. "But I'm sure you do."

After the long night, dawn finally arrived—a pale pink stripe in the darkness just above the horizon. And suddenly it was full day. The city was alive again. Sofia could hear buses and cars in the distance, and a radio was playing inside a house.

Finally a woman arrived. She was big and fat. She stopped in front of Sofia where she sat in her wheel-chair.

"Who are you?" she asked. "Why are you sitting here?"

"My name is Sofia. I arrived yesterday."

The woman shook her head.

"But you weren't supposed to come until today. Have you been sitting here all night?"

Sofia nodded.

The woman clapped her hands angrily.

"That hospital is so disorganized!" she said. "How can they come and simply leave you here a day early?"

"I don't know," Sofia said.

"And you've been sitting here all night?"

"Yes," Sofia said.

"Poor girl," said the woman. "Let me show you where you're going to live. Then you'll get some food. My name is Veronica and I work here."

Veronica took a firm grip of the wheelchair and started pushing. The crooked wheels lurched across the uneven yard. They went through a gate into another compound. There was a rectangular build-ing with a verandah and a long row of open doors. Veronica pushed the wheelchair. There was someone sitting outside every door. Sofia noticed that they were all old and ill. Many had dirty bandages around various parts of their bodies; others were missing legs or hands or fingers. There was a bad smell and Sofia wondered what she was doing there.

At the end of the verandah Veronica stopped outside a closed door. "This is where you'll be living," she said, and opened the door.

Sofia looked into the dark room. There were two old steel beds without mattresses.

"Am I going to live here on my own?" Sofia asked.

"When you've learned how to walk, you can go home to your mama," Veronica said. "You'll get something to eat soon."

Sofia lowered herself down from the wheelchair. It was as if she'd become little again, as she'd been before she learned to walk. She crawled over the doorsill and sat on the floor looking around. There was nothing in the room apart from the beds. A piece of wood covered a hole in the wall where a window had been. A rat scurried out from a corner and disappeared through the door.

Sofia slid across to the bed. The moment she'd arrived in the room she knew she wouldn't be able to crawl because that would have torn the bandages. The only way she could get around was to slide on her backside. She managed to get herself up onto the bed and lay down on the rusty steel springs. They rubbed at her back and neck, but she was so exhausted after the long night in the wheelchair that she was too tired to think, and she fell asleep right away.

When she woke up, her whole body was aching. On the floor beside her bed there was a plate with cold maize porridge and a piece of pork rind. She slid down onto the floor and took the plate with her to the doorway. An old man without eyes went past outside the door. She watched him as he disappeared through a door at the far end of the building. Sofia guessed that was where she should go when she needed a toilet.

She was hungry, but the food tasted so awful that she had to force herself to eat it. It might be forbidden to leave food on the plate. Maybe they'd punish her by making her sit in the wheelchair for another night.

When she finished, she put the plate aside and stayed sitting in the doorway. She looked sadly at her dirty bandages.

Sofia didn't want to live in the dark room. She wanted to go home to Mama Lydia and Alfredo, even if she couldn't walk. Why should she live here with a lot of old, sick people she didn't know?

There isn't even a fire here, she thought. There are no flames that I can sit and stare into.

They haven't taken only my legs away from me.

They've also taken the secrets in the fire.

How long she stayed sitting there in the doorway, she didn't know. When Veronica came waddling to fetch the empty plate, she could tell that Sofia was miserable. Although she had lots to do—because it was she who did the cooking for everyone that lived in the home, for the old and the poor and the ill—she sat down, drew Sofia close, and held her.

"Right now you're unhappy," she said. "You have no legs, you can't walk. Your sister is gone and you don't know anyone here. You're wondering what's going to happen. And you had to sit all by yourself for a whole night in your wheelchair. The food doesn't taste too good either, even though I do the best I can with the little I've got. You're sad and you have no idea what's going on. Am I right?"

Sofia was firmly held in Veronica's big arms. She answered with a feeble nod. But she felt comfortable. She could feel Veronica's heart.

"It'll be easier in a couple of days," Veronica said. "And you must learn how to walk again. You need to stay here so you can get your new legs."

When she left, Sofia felt slightly better. Not a lot, but it was something.

The following morning, Veronica woke her early. Sofia's body ached from sleeping on the steel springs. At one stage during the night, she'd woken up when a rat ran across her body.

"If only you just had a mattress to lie on," Veronica said. "But we have nothing here. We should be thankful there's food."

Sofia slid across to the pump in the yard and washed herself. Then she crawled into the wheelchair. Veronica wheeled her to the outer yard, where a car came to pick her up.

At the hospital, Sofia was taken to a large hall with mirrors along one of the walls. On the floor there were a variety of large, wooden frames, with people of all ages using them to learn to walk for the second time in their lives. Most of the patients had only one artificial leg; a few had two. Sofia sat in her wheelchair watching them. Would she ever be able to learn?

Suddenly someone tapped her on the shoulder. When she turned around she saw Master Emilio smiling at her.

"Now's the time," he said, holding up two wooden sticks. There was a strap at the top and a shoe at the bottom of each one.

"You'll be starting with these practise legs," he said. "First of all, your knees need to get used to the fact that they're getting new legs. It'll hurt in the beginning. You'll get sores. But the sores will heal in a couple of months."

While Master Emilio was talking, another man in a white coat had joined them. He was much younger than Master Emilio.

"This is Benthino," Master Emilio said. "He's the one who'll be helping you until you can walk again."

Benthino smiled at her.

"Sofia," he said. "We must become friends. We'll be seeing each other every day for a long time."

"Yes," Sofia said.

They strapped the two sticks onto her legs. Then they lifted her out of the chair. She felt the pain in her stumps. But at the same time she felt like singing: she was standing again! Benthino gave her two crutches.

"Try to take a step," he said. "You won't fall. You've got your crutches. And I'm here. If you do fall, I'll catch you."

"How do I do it?" Sofia said.

"Just the same as usual," Benthino said. "Don't think about the fact that they're a couple of legs made of wood. Just walk the way you did before."

Sofia took one step. It felt stiff and unfamiliar. It was like the time when she'd tried to walk on stilts. Her stumps hurt and the straps around her thighs pinched and rubbed. Benthino let go of her, and he and Master Emilio went to stand against the opposite wall.

"Come over here," he called. "Walk slowly. You won't fall."

"I can't," Sofia answered.

"You can," said Benthino.

She tried to take a step. It was like lifting something

heavy that hung from her body. First one leg, then the other. *In her mind's eye she can see herself and Maria running along the path.* Next leg. Lift it, put it in front of the other. *They are running. They are playing. It's a new game that Sofia has invented.* Next leg. One step forward. Lean on the crutches, find her balance. *They are going to run with their eyes shut. She does what she usually does when she invents a new game. She tries it herself first. Then she tells Maria how to do it.* Next step. The wooden stick with the black shoe up into the air and forward, crutches on the floor. *She closes her eyes and runs. But the path is wet. She slips and trips; can't stop.* Next leg. The crutch forward, then the leg, lift her body, keep her balance. *She opens her eyes. She's off the path. She's standing on one leg and turns around and sees Maria. She knows she's not supposed to put her foot down. But it's too late.*

Sofia fell.

Benthino laughed. He and Emilio picked her up, gathered the crutches, tightened a strap that had come loose. Suddenly they noticed that Sofia had tears in her eyes.

"Did you hurt yourself?" Benthino asked.

"We were just playing," Sofia said. "I tripped."

Benthino didn't understand what she meant. He wanted her to keep walking. But Master Emilio put a hand on his arm and said that Sofia needed to rest.

He'd seen this before. He could sense that this was the first time Sofia had remembered what happened when the landmine exploded.

"We won't walk anymore today," he said. "Doctor Raul told me you liked to sit out on the street."

Sofia nodded. She only half heard what he said. She was thinking about what had happened, and what she had only just understood. It had been a landmine. She had been playing. She'd had her eyes closed while she was running.

It was she who had stepped on the mine.

It was her fault that Maria died.

Sofia went cold. Only monsters killed other people.

Master Emilio wheeled her out onto the street.

"Benthino will come and get you when it's time to go home," he said. "Sit here in the sun and get warm."

Miranda was there, and all the other women. But Sofia didn't want to talk to anyone. She pulled the blanket over her head. She wanted to be invisible.

She was sitting like that when Benthino came to fetch her. She didn't reply when he asked why she was sitting underneath the blanket. Even after the car had driven her out to the old people's home and Veronica had wheeled her to her room, she still sat with her head under the blanket. She didn't want any food. Not until she had slid into her room and closed the door did she remove the blanket from her head. She felt totally empty, as empty as the dark room where she sat. All she could think was that she didn't want to live anymore. It was her fault that Maria was dead.

I'll never leave this room, she thought. I'll sit here on the floor until I'm old.

Evening fell. Veronica brought a plate of food. But Sofia threw the blanket over her head and didn't reply when Veronica asked if she wasn't hungry. Veronica left and closed the door behind her. Sofia didn't even bother to remove the blanket. She sat on the floor without moving, waiting to grow old.

The door opened again. She thought it was Veronica coming back again.

But something was different. It didn't sound like Veronica's footsteps. Sofia sat under the blanket trying to work out who it was. She heard the person sit down on the other bed. She also heard a candle being lit, and smelled smoke and wax through the blanket. Finally, Sofia couldn't control her curiosity any longer and she removed the blanket.

On the other bed sat a girl about her own age. Sofia saw that one of her legs was missing—the left one.

They looked at each other.

"My name is Hortensia," said the girl. "What's yours?"

"Sofia."

"Have you lost a leg, too?"

"Both of them."

They were silent again. They looked at each other.

"Why were you sitting under the blanket?" the girl asked.

Sofia didn't answer. She didn't know what to say.

"I'm going to live here," said Hortensia, "while I'm at the hospital learning to walk with a new leg."

Sofia couldn't believe it. Was she really not going to have to live by herself anymore?

"How long are you staying here?" she asked.

"I don't know," Hortensia answered. "A long time, probably."

From that moment, everything was different. Sofia no longer had to be alone.

Hortensia and Sofia became friends. Sofia sometimes thought it was like getting a new sister. Hortensia could never replace Maria, but everything was so much easier now that she was there. At night, Sofia lay listening to Hortensia breathe, and knew that she would still be there in the morning. They went to the hospital together, they practised together, they sat outside together with the women selling oranges. They braided each other's hair, they invented songs, and they talked about everything that went on around them.

Hortensia had stepped on a landmine, too. She came from far away—so far that her mother could never come and visit.

"You can borrow my mama," Sofia said. "Lydia has enough room for you, too."

It was true. When Lydia came to visit and saw how happy Sofia was, she immediately began treating Hortensia as if she were her own daughter.

The days passed quickly. Although it was difficult practising how to walk with new legs, both girls noticed it got easier and easier. One day Sofia discovered she could even manage with just one crutch. Master Emilio came from time to time to check their progress. He promised that their legs would soon be ready.

One evening, Sofia told Hortensia how it had been her fault that Maria died.

Hortensia shook her head.

"You couldn't possibly have known there was a landmine there," she said. "It wasn't your fault. It was the mine's fault."

When she heard Hortensia put it like that, Sofia resolved never to sit under the blanket again.

They talked about everything. But there was one subject they never mentioned: they knew that one day they would have to part. Hortensia would go home, and Sofia would go home. For Sofia, the thought was unbearable. She didn't want to lose Hortensia, like she'd lost Maria. Although Hortensia would still be alive, it amounted to the same thing. They would never see each other again.

Learning how to walk again went easier for Hortensia, who needed only one new leg. It was a lot harder for Sofia, and she was sometimes envious that Hortensia had lost only one of her legs. But she kept her envy to herself. Sofia never told anyone how she felt.

One day, when they'd arrived home and were sitting in the doorway waiting for their meal, a man came and told Hortensia that she didn't need to practise anymore, and that her new leg was ready. She was to pack her few belongings and leave right away. He was there to drive her to a bus that would take her home.

They barely had time to say goodbye. Everything happened so fast. They clumsily touched hands, and then Hortensia made her way out into the yard.

Sofia sat in the doorway and watched her leave. Hortensia turned the corner and was gone.

Sofia closed the door behind her.

She was alone again.

CHAPTER EIGHT

SOFIA NEVER FORGOT Hortensia.

But she never saw her again.

Every morning, when she woke up, she was reminded that Hortensia had gone. Her bed stood empty. Sofia asked Veronica whether another girl would come. But Veronica didn't know.

The bed remained empty.

The days passed, slowly and heavily. Sofia sometimes thought about time and how it both existed and didn't exist, and how it was like the lazy hippopotamuses she used to see floating in the river when she and Maria washed their clothes.

Sofia wanted to learn how to walk so she could go home as soon as possible, but she also wondered what the future held. She would never be able to run or dance. And no man would want her when she was ready to have children.

Her thoughts would have been less heavy if she'd

had someone to share them with, but Hortensia was gone for good.

One day, Sofia's new legs were ready. Doctor Raul came to fetch her from the hall where she practised walking with Benthino. Together they went to Master Emilio. He smiled at her and pointed to two legs that stood leaning against the table.

"May I introduce you to your two new friends?" he said. "They'll be with you for many years to come. Since you're still growing, you'll be needing new and longer legs at some stage, but until then these are your best friends."

The legs were made of light brown plastic. They were the same thickness as normal legs and had black shoes at the end. One of the legs was longer than the other, since it had to be fastened to her thigh.

Together Master Emilio and Doctor Raul attached Sofia's new legs. When she stood up, she felt how well they fit her. It only hurt a little bit below her left knee. If she let her *capulana* fall all the way down to her shoes, no one would notice that her legs weren't really her own.

Doctor Raul told her to walk around the room.

"Does it hurt?" he asked.

Sofia shook her head.

"Can I go home now?" she asked.

"Not yet," said Doctor Raul. "You will need at least

another month here, to practise. But then you can go home."

That night, Sofia tried out different ways of arranging her *capulana* so that the artificial legs couldn't be seen. She walked back and forth outside the building, and it was almost as if nothing had happened. People who didn't know wouldn't be able to tell that her legs were made of plastic.

From then on, Sofia no longer used the wheelchair. Before, she'd always put on her legs when she got to the hospital, but now she did it in the morning and kept them on until she went to bed at night. She took them to bed with her, too, and kept them under the blanket, because she was afraid someone might try to steal them.

One night, as she lay in bed with the legs beside her, she thought she would give them each a name. If Doctor Raul was right about them being her best friends, they had to be called something. She lay in the darkness thinking. What could you call a couple of legs? After thinking back and forth for some time, she called the right leg Kukula and the left leg Xitsongo. The names meant "short" and "long" in her language.

She also decided not to tell anyone about the names that she'd given her legs. Old Muazena once told her that your secrets are safest and best kept if you sit by a fire and throw your thoughts into the flames like firewood. Then they would always be there, even when the fire burned low and died. They'd come alive again when the fire was relit the next day.

"The fire won't betray you," Muazena had said. "It keeps your secrets and never reveals them to anyone."

During this period, Mama Lydia and José-Maria came to visit less and less often. They were busy, and Sofia often sat in the doorway waiting in vain for them to come. Sometimes she was so homesick it hurt. There was nothing she found more difficult to endure. If she didn't get food one night she could sleep off her hunger, but homesickness was worse.

More often now, Doctor Raul would give her a couple of banknotes. She usually bought an orange with the money, but one day she had an idea. If she saved the money, it might add up to enough for a seat on one of the rusty old trucks that drove people back and forth between the city and the outlying villages. She would surprise her mama and Alfredo by coming home for a weekend, when she wasn't at the hospital practising with her new legs. She knew she lived near Boane. Once she got that far, she'd be able to find her way home.

She asked Veronica where she might find the trucks

that took people to Boane. To make sure that Veronica wouldn't suspect that she was thinking of going there—and maybe tell her she wasn't allowed—Sofia tried to ask as if she wasn't really interested in the answer. Veronica explained, and Sofia remembered everything she said.

After about a week, she had saved enough money. She decided to leave early on Saturday morning. To make sure Veronica wouldn't worry, she would tell one of the old fellows who was always up early that she'd gone home and that she'd be back on Sunday. She had also saved some of the bread she got at mealtimes, and hidden it in a piece of paper in her bed.

Sofia grew more and more anxious as the day of her departure neared. What if she got into the wrong truck? If that happened, she might end up in a strange place and be unable to find her way back. And she didn't know how long the trip would take, either.

But she'd made up her mind. She had to go home.

The night before she left, she slept poorly. As she had no way of telling the time, she could never work out how long it would be until sunrise. When she couldn't bear to lie in bed any longer, she got up, attached her legs, and got dressed. Carefully she opened the door into the darkness. It was warm and still. She could hear snoring and coughing from the other rooms where the old people lay asleep. Sofia sat in the door-way to wait for the sun. She had knotted the money and the pieces of bread into a corner of her *capulana,* and while she waited she thought through Veronica's directions for finding a truck to Boane.

At last she caught a glimpse of the first pale streak of dawn. A door opened further along the verandah. A blind old man called Manuel crept out and sat in the doorway. It was time to leave. Sofia helped herself up with her crutch, closed the door, and set off. When she passed Manuel she said good morning and asked him to tell Veronica that she'd gone home.

"You should be glad you have a home," Manuel said. "All I have is this. No family, nothing."

Sofia felt sorry for old Manuel. She wondered what was worse—to have two artificial legs, or to be blind.

She walked as fast as she could, because she wanted to be gone from the compound by the time Veronica arrived. Of course, there was also the risk of meeting her on the road, since she didn't know from which direction Veronica would be coming.

It was daylight when Sofia left the main gate, and many people were already on their way to work. She followed the dusty road in the direction Veronica had described.

The chapa *towards Boane leaves from the market-place outside the cathedral. First you turn to the left,*

*then to the right, and then just continue straight ahead,
down the long hill.*

Sofia turned left and then right. Whenever she
crossed a street, the cars beeped their horns at her.
But she went as fast as she could. Angrily she told
Xitsongo and Kukula to hurry up. From time to time
she had to stop to catch her breath. What if it was so
far that she couldn't manage the walk? She set off
again, afraid that she might have gone the wrong way.
The sun was already high in the sky; sweat ran from
her face. But she clenched her teeth and kept going.
She wasn't going to give up; she had to go home.

At last she arrived. At the far end of the market-
place was a big white church with a steeple. Trucks
were parked along the pavement with people clambering off and on. Other trucks arrived, packed with
people clinging to the sides for support. The drivers
nudged their way forwards slowly because they had
so many people on board. Sofia wondered how she
would ever manage to get up onto one of those high
trucks. And if she did manage, how would she get off
again when the truck arrived in Boane? But she
pushed her fears aside. She couldn't give up now.
Manuel had probably already told Veronica that Sofia
had gone home. She couldn't change her mind.

Sofia approached a woman who was sitting on the
pavement with a cage full of hens in front of her. She
asked about the trucks to Boane. The woman pointed

and asked why Sofia was using crutches. Had she fallen and hurt herself? Sofia nodded. She went in the direction the woman had indicated. The woman hadn't noticed that Sofia had artificial legs. She was glad, and the thought gave her new strength. There was a boy hanging from a truck door calling out to customers, and Sofia asked if he was heading for Boane.

"Matola and Boane," he yelled back. "Two thousand."

Sofia was stunned. Two thousand. She didn't have that much. She only had fifteen hundred.

"I've only got fifteen hundred," Sofia shouted to him.

"Then you have to get off outside Matola," he answered, and started taking money from other people who were clambering onto the truck. Sofia was jostled back and forth, and almost fell over several times. She tried to call out to the boy again but he didn't see her: he was busy with the people climbing onto his truck. It would soon be completely full. Sofia didn't know what to do—she only knew that she had to get onto that truck.

Suddenly someone touched her. She started and turned around. She recognized one of the nurses from the time she had spent in the hospital room. Her name was Laurinda.

"Sofia," she said. "Where are you going?"

"I'm going home," Sofia said. "But I'm five hundred short."

"I'll give you the money," Laurinda said. "Some time, when you have the money, you can pay me back."

"Are you going to Boane too?" Sofia asked.

Laurinda smiled.

"I'm going to the hospital," she said. "I've just arrived."

The boy hanging from the truck door started shouting that the truck was about to leave. Laurinda yelled that Sofia was coming and asked the passengers crowding on the back of the truck to help her up. Someone took her crutches, and then she felt strong arms lifting her. She couldn't do anything about the *capulana* being pulled up. As she hung there in the air, many people saw that she had artificial legs. Sofia was squeezed in between the mass of people, and someone handed her crutches back. The boy reached out and got his money. A few more people climbed on board with baskets and boxes and even a bleating goat. Then the truck jerked into motion. Sofia didn't need to use her crutches for support—she was tightly pressed between two fat women balancing baskets on their heads.

Sofia was delighted to be surrounded by so many people. She didn't want to think about the loneliness she'd suffered for such a long time.

A fresh breeze blew about her head. The truck swayed and jolted and turned. As soon as they reached the outskirts of the city, the pace picked up. From time to time the truck stopped to let people off and take new passengers on. She asked one of the fat women how much further it was to Boane.

"First we cross the bridge," the woman said. "Then we go up a hill. And down a hill. And then we're there."

Sofia closed her eyes and felt the wind on her face. She should have been worrying about how she would find home once she got off the truck in Boane, and how she would get back to the city without money for the return ticket. But she didn't want to think about it. Muazena had told her that among the secrets in the fire were the solutions to problems. Somewhere, surely, Sofia would be able to find a burning fire where she could sit down and look into the flames.

The truck braked and pulled over to the side of the road. They had arrived. Lots of people were getting off and Sofia was jostled from all sides. She threw the crutches to the ground and strong arms helped her down from the truck. She knew which direction to go in. The sun was beating down, so she wrapped a piece of fabric around her head and started walking.

The crutches sank in the gravel and the going was difficult, but she clenched her teeth and struggled on. She knew it was a long way. In the bright glare of the sun, she could see the outline of the mountains on the horizon. They made her feel at home. Those were the mountains she and Maria had always seen when they ran to the fields in the mornings.

When she had walked herself to a sweat, she stopped in the shade of a tree and ate her piece of bread. She regretted that she hadn't brought any water and knew she would be very thirsty by the time she got home. Her thighs and left knee hurt, but she didn't have time to rest in the shade; she had to keep going. From time to time a car passed, but no one stopped to ask if she needed a lift.

Sofia didn't arrive in the village until late in the afternoon. By then she was almost dropping with fatigue and thirst. There was a well on the outskirts of the village, and she'd been longing for it for several hours. When she finally reached it there were a number of women and children with plastic containers waiting their turn to get water. Many of them recognized Sofia—including many who had believed that she was dead and who were now overjoyed to see her again. They gave her water to drink and she sat down on the edge of the well to catch her breath. Someone gave her a fruit and they all asked about the city and wanted to see her legs. Someone also ran over to Lydia's hut to tell her that Sofia had come home.

Sofia had already left the well to walk the last stretch when she saw Lydia approaching with Alfredo. Lydia seemed almost frightened to see her.

She stroked her arms and asked if she'd been sent away from the hospital.

"I just wanted to say hello," Sofia said. "I have to leave again tomorrow."

"Did you walk all the way?" Lydia asked. "It must have taken you several days."

"I came on a truck," Sofia said. "I bought a ticket."

She didn't mention that she had no money for the return ticket. That would just have worried Lydia even more. Sofia never understood why adults worried about problems that would come later on, some other day.

When they got home and Sofia sat herself on the straw mat, she was so exhausted that all she wanted to do was lie down. But people kept coming to visit; everyone wanted to say hello to her. Again and again she had to tell about her time in the hospital, about the big city, and show off her legs. She forgot she was tired and felt the joy of being home among the people she knew. Lydia started cooking, and Alfredo sat by Sofia's side and stared at her with big eyes.

Sofia noticed that Mama Lydia had grown thick around the middle, which meant she would soon be having a child, and Sofia would be getting a new brother or sister. She wondered which one of the men who came visiting was the child's father, but she didn't want to ask. She would find out soon enough. The idea of having another sibling made her happy because it meant that everything was well with Mama Lydia.

That night they stayed up by the fire longer than usual. People kept appearing out of the shadows and coming forward to say hello. Alfredo fell asleep next to her and at last there were only Lydia and Sofia left by the fire.

"When are you coming home for good?" Lydia asked.

"I don't know," Sofia answered. "Soon, I hope."

"You shouldn't have come on a truck all the way here," Lydia said. "Who gave you money for the ticket?"

"Doctor Raul."

"What if you can't find your way back?"

"The trucks follow the road," Sofia answered. "And the road leads to the city. I can't get lost."

When Lydia carried Alfredo inside, Sofia said that she wanted to sit by the fire a little longer before she went to bed. Lydia didn't ask why, and disappeared into the hut.

Sofia was alone. As she sat there, staring into the flames, she realized that her homesickness was as much due to wanting to meet the fire as to anything else. Now, for the first time—as she sat in the warm darkness outside the hut, listening to drums thumping in the distance—she could think seriously about everything that had happened. And it wasn't only Muazena and Hapakatanda's faces she thought she could see faintly in the flames. Now Maria's face was there too. Maria, who was now somewhere among the dead. It gave Sofia a sense of relief to think that Maria had Muazena and Hapakatanda close to her.

It was as if she could hear Maria's voice. She was saying that it wasn't Sofia's fault that she was dead. No one could have known there would be a mine at the very place where Sofia placed her right foot. It wasn't her fault.

When Sofia finally went to bed, the fire had burned down to smouldering coals. Maybe it had been to hear Maria's voice from among the flames that she'd come home? If that was true, then she had made the right decision—in which case, Veronica would have no right to be angry with her.

The next day, Sofia discovered she need not have worried about finding money for the trip back. José-Maria heard that Sofia had come for a visit and turned up on the road. He crouched down next to her and smiled.

"I knew you'd get through this," he said. "You'll be able to come back again soon."

Then he said the best thing of all.

"I'm going to the city this afternoon. You can come with me."

In the afternoon, Lydia gave Sofia a basket of vegetables. Then José-Maria arrived with his car and it was time to leave. Sofia said goodbye and looked at the black remains of the fire.

"I'll be back soon, Maria," she whispered.

That evening, back in her lonely room, she felt things would be easier now that she knew she would soon be going home for good.

Not only that, but she had talked to Maria. Maria was with Muazena and Hapakatanda. She would be safe there. As safe as you can be when you are dead.

The worst part was over—her worries, her loneliness. She patted Kukula and Xitsongo where they lay next to her on the bed.

They really had become her best friends.

CHAPTER NINE

ONE DAY, the training was over.

Sofia realized that time—time that seemed to both exist and not exist—had surprised her again. In the end, time had passed so quickly that she hadn't even thought about it.

Master Emilio and Doctor Raul came into the hall where she was walking back and forth under the watchful eye of Benthino. They stood watching her and then, when she sat down for a rest, they said she didn't need to practise any longer. She could now go home without having to come back.

Sofia was confused. Could it really be true? Was her long loneliness over?

"Your new friends are taking good care of you already," Doctor Raul said, pointing to her legs.

"In a few years you'll have to come back," Master Emilio said. "But not until you've grown so much that you need new legs."

"I can't teach her anymore," Benthino said. "I have many people waiting in line to learn how to walk."

"I'll drive you home myself," said Doctor Raul. "Tomorrow I'll come and pick you up from the home where you're staying."

That day, several of the nurses who had taken care of Sofia during that first difficult time came to greet her, including Marta, Celeste, and Mariza. Sofia felt shy and didn't know what to say. In the afternoon, just before the car came to fetch her, she hurried outside, hopping on her crutches, to the women who sat on the street selling their goods. Miranda was there, and so were all the others. When Sofia told them she was going home a loud racket broke out. They all talked and shouted at once, and wished her good luck. Sofia felt shy all over again.

When she got back to the home for the old and the sick, the hardest part was yet to come. She had to say goodbye to Veronica, who had been so helpful and had been like her second mother for such a long time. Sofia would miss her in a special way, almost in the way she missed those who'd been left behind in the burned village they'd once fled. But Veronica just seemed to be happy for Sofia, that she could finally go home.

"I'm sure you'll come by to say hello," she said.

Sofia nodded but she wondered whether that would ever happen. Now that she was leaving the city she found it difficult to imagine that she would ever come back. She'd never become used to the tall buildings, to the many cars and the multitudes of strangers.

Sofia wanted to live among people who had names and who would be her friends even if they weren't members of her family. Once, long ago, when they had still been running away, she had thought that the city would be something exciting. It was something she had longed to see in the same way that she'd longed to see the ocean. But there was a difference between the ocean and the city. The difference was inside her. She wanted to leave the city, but she wanted to see the ocean again.

She also remembered the old woman they'd met while they were fleeing—the one who'd sat down one day and never got up again. "We don't have legs that are made to walk to the city," she had said. Even so, Sofia had gone to the city after all—and it was to get new legs!

She collected her few belongings and sat in the doorway to watch the sun set. In every doorway along the verandah she saw heads and huddled bodies. Most of them were old men, weak and blind, who were missing an arm or a leg. Many of them had leprosy and would probably never leave. They had nowhere to go, no place to return to.

For the very last time, Veronica arrived with a plate. Sofia ate and Veronica sat beside her in the doorway.

"Who will live here after me?" Sofia asked.

"There'll always be someone," Veronica answered.

There had been something on Sofia's mind all afternoon. She thought that now was the time to mention it to Veronica.

"If Hortensia comes back," she said, "say hello to her from me."

For a moment it looked as though Veronica didn't remember who Hortensia was. But suddenly she nodded.

"Hortensia," she said. "I'd almost forgotten her. But if she comes back, of course I'll say hello from you."

Dusk fell. It grew dark. Sofia couldn't wait for morning to come so that she could go home with Doctor Raul, and she fell asleep early that night

The next day, she left the city. Doctor Raul came to pick her up. It was the first time she'd seen him without his white doctor's coat. His car was small and old. The bumper hung from a wire, one of the headlights was gone and, when Sofia got in, the car wouldn't start. Doctor Raul waved his arms in despair. Then he swore. Although he looked angry, Sofia couldn't help laughing. They got help from some boys to push-start the car. Sofia thought it was strange that a doctor, who probably had plenty of money, had such an old and useless car, but she didn't say anything.

Doctor Raul sat behind the wheel and sang. From time to time he shouted at other drivers when he thought they'd done something wrong.

At one stage, when they had stopped at a red light, he turned and smiled at her.

"I'm off today," he said, "and that's why I can drive you home. Today I'm your private *motorista*."

They left the city. As they passed the open fields, Sofia saw women bending over their hoes and longed to have soil on her hands again. She wished she could sing along with Doctor Raul, but she didn't dare. So she sang inside instead.

At the top of a hill they got a puncture. The car suddenly started shaking and Doctor Raul pulled over to the side of the road. He got out and walked around the car. Sofia peered through the car window and saw him kick one of the back tires.

"Do you know how to change tires on a car?" he asked. "I have no idea."

Sofia shook her head.

Although getting in and out of cars was hard for her, she opened the door, leaned on one of the crutches, and managed to get herself out onto the road without falling over. Meanwhile, Doctor Raul was rummaging through the trunk in search of the spare tire and his tools. His white shirt was already dirty.

"I can operate on human beings," he said. "But I can't change the tires on a car."

"I can't operate or change tires," Sofia said. Then she waved one of her crutches at a passing car.

"What are you doing?" Doctor Raul asked.

"If you can't do something yourself, you should ask someone else to help you," Sofia said.

She waved with the crutch again. A car pulled over behind them. A man got out and asked what had happened. Then he changed the tire. Sofia watched with interest. If she was ever going to go somewhere in Doctor Raul's old car again she'd better learn how to change a flat tire. Doctor Raul wanted to pay the man for his help, but he just waved his arms and grinned.

"Maybe I'll operate on you one day," Doctor Raul said.

"I'd rather not," the man said. "I'm not ill."

Sofia got into the backseat again and the man helped to push the car.

It wasn't long before they reached Boane and turned off the main road. They drove over the Impamputo River. The bridge was narrow, and Doctor Raul had to wait until a herd of goats had crossed. Sofia watched children playing in the water. Further away, a naked man stood washing himself and, at the foot of the bridge, some women were washing clothes. Sofia looked at everything that was going on and thought, I can do that. I can do that. And that. And that.

There were really only a few things she would never be able to do again—like dance and run.

That made her sad—especially the fact that she could never dance. To run wasn't so important, but never to stand with the other women in a circle and dance...

There was one other thought in her head, a thought she almost didn't dare to think. What would happen when she grew older? Would there be a man who would want to marry her in spite of her artificial legs, and despite the fact that she couldn't dance? Would she be able to have children? Or would she live her whole life without ever being able to carry her own child on her back?

She didn't want to think about it. That would be tempting fate.

They had left the river behind them. The road was now narrow and full of holes. Doctor Raul had rolled up the window so that the whirling dust wouldn't get in. Sofia knew she must have traveled this road before, in the opposite direction, although she couldn't remember it. After the accident. She had so many questions that she wanted answered. There was still so much she didn't know.

They arrived on the outskirts of the village.

"You'll have to show me the way now," Doctor Raul said. "I can't find my way from here."

Sofia showed him where to drive and before long they had arrived at her home. But to Sofia's disappointment there was no one around. One of the neighbors came to greet her. She realized that Mama Lydia must be out working on the fields, and asked after Alfredo.

"Alfredo is with your mother today," the neighbor said.

Doctor Raul stood beside the car looking thoughtfully at the hut where Sofia lived. He looked at the cracked straw walls and knew that when the rains came they would be lying on a damp dirt floor with rain dripping through the bad roof. Sofia came from a poor family, the poorest of the poor. Still, he knew she was happy to be home.

Sofia is strong, he thought. She'll manage.

Even so, he felt sad about the life that lay ahead of her. A life filled with struggle. The life of the poor.

He said goodbye to Sofia.

"I hope everything goes well," he said. "When I have the time, I'll come and visit you."

Sofia looked down shyly. She was almost ashamed to have caused Doctor Raul so much trouble. He'd had to stoop over her to operate. Surely he had more important people to take care of.

She waved as he drove off.

She wondered if she would ever see him again.

For the rest of the day, Sofia sat in the shade of the tree beside the hut, enjoying being home. From time to time somebody would stop on the road and look at her as if they couldn't believe their eyes. Then they'd come across to her and she would have to describe what had happened to her, and show off her new legs, over and over again. Every time a new person asked to hear what had happened since the accident, she noticed that she told them less and less. She would rather they didn't ask anything at all.

It would have been better if everyone forgot. That is, everyone apart from herself. Because she couldn't forget. If she forgot, then she would forget Maria, too. And that was never going to happen.

Never, for as long as she lived.

It was already late in the afternoon when Sofia finally saw Lydia on the road. Alfredo was running along beside her. Sofia got up from the ground and waved. Alfredo saw her first. He tugged at Lydia's arm and pointed.

Then Sofia noticed that Lydia was carrying a child on her back. She'd completely forgotten that Lydia was going to have a baby. She could feel her chest swell with happiness. A new family member. Was it a brother or a sister?

They hugged each other. Lydia stroked her, but Alfredo stayed in the background, shy to be seeing Sofia again. Then Lydia took the child off her back and handed it to Sofia, who sat down again.

"Your brother," Lydia said and smiled. Sofia noticed that Lydia had lost several of her teeth.

Sofia took her brother. He was sleeping and was barely a month old. How long ago had it been since Sofia last saw Lydia? The days had all run together. She held her brother in her arms and felt great happiness.

"What's his name?" she asked.

"Faustino," Lydia said. "His father will come when we're ready to eat."

At last there would be an answer to Sofia's curiosity. She would soon meet Lydia's new man. It was an important moment. She noticed herself getting nervous, but she was glad at the same time. Everything would be so much easier with a man in the house.

Lydia began preparing dinner while Sofia sat holding her brother.

"I can't believe you're back," Lydia said, over and over again. "I can't believe you finally came back."

Then Lydia turned serious. Sofia knew that she could switch from happy to serious faster than any person she knew.

"But how are you going to manage?" she asked.

At first Sofia didn't understand what Lydia meant.

"I can walk again," she said.

Lydia shook her head but she didn't say anything else. Sofia felt a pain in her stomach. What did Lydia mean? Why shouldn't she manage?

She never finished the thought.

A man suddenly appeared. They hadn't noticed him approaching in the shadows beyond Sofia.

Alfredo ran into the hut.

Sofia immediately sensed that Alfredo was afraid of the man who'd arrived. The man was tall and solid. Sofia could tell from his breath that he'd been drinking *tontonto,* a homemade liquor. He gave her such a piercing stare that she looked away.

"Who is this?" he asked.

Sofia stole a look at him as he gestured to Lydia to get up from the fire where she was cooking.

"This is my daughter, Sofia," Lydia answered.

Sofia almost didn't recognize her mother's voice. It was different, weaker, as though someone had hit her.

The man took a step closer to Sofia.

"So this is the one who was clumsy enough to step on a landmine?" he said.

Sofia went cold.

"And now she's come back," said the man. "Now she's here and wants to be fed. She'll be walking with crutches for the rest of her life."

The man disappeared around the back of the hut for a moment.

"Don't take any notice of what he says," Lydia whispered. "He says a lot of things when he's been drinking. Apart from that, he's nice."

"Is that my stepfather?" Sofia asked.

Lydia nodded. Then she hurried back to the fire so that the food wouldn't burn.

Alfredo peeked warily from the doorway. Sofia could see he was scared of his stepfather, Faustino's father.

Sofia's stomach hurt more and more. Why had Lydia found herself a man who was mean? Why wasn't he happy to see her? Why did he say that she'd been clumsy when she stepped on the mine? But she tried to believe that what Lydia said was true. It was only when he'd been drinking *tontonto* that he was mean. It was only then that Alfredo was afraid.

But deep inside she had a feeling it wasn't like that. Much later, several full moons later, she would understand that on that very first night, she had known she wouldn't be able to stay.

The moment Lydia's new man emerged from the shadows at the back of the hut, Sofia lost her home. Lydia's man wanted Lydia, but not her children. Sofia had heard about this sort of thing before, about stepfathers who threw out the children women brought from previous husbands. But she had never thought it would happen to Lydia.

The next moment she was ashamed of her thoughts. Maybe it was true, after all, what Lydia had said. That it was only when he'd been drinking *tontonto* that he was mean.

They ate dinner in silence. Alfredo sat as far from the fire as he could, hiding in the darkness near Sofia. Lydia called the man "Isaias." Sofia got the impression that Lydia, too, was scared of him. She couldn't understand why Lydia had chosen a man who didn't like her children, a man she was afraid of. She no longer recognized her mother. What had happened to her? She remembered how Lydia used to be, full of strength and joy, always talking, laughing, dancing, working. Now she sat hunched, her face seemed to have shrunk, and her teeth had started to fall out of her mouth.

When they'd eaten, Isaias went into the hut without a word. Before long they heard him snoring.

"Is he going to live here?" Sofia asked.

"He's going to look after us," Lydia answered. "You have to obey him, as you obey me."

"What does he do?" Sofia asked.

"He doesn't have a job," Lydia said, "but he's trying to find something to do to make money."

"How is he going to be able to help us if he doesn't work?"

Sofia couldn't hide her sadness and anger. The joy of coming home had vanished. Life would only get harder with Isaias. How was she going to obey a man who clearly didn't like her?

"I don't think he should live here," Sofia said.

Lydia was angry.

"Are you going to tell me what to do?" she yelled. "I've finally found a new man, we already have a child together, and you are arguing with me!"

Then she started crying. Sofia regretted having spoken to Lydia in that way. She couldn't know what it had been like for Lydia to live so long without Hapakatanda. She decided maybe it was good after all that Isaias was going to live with them.

But Isaias drank every day. On several occasions he hit Alfredo. Lydia seemed to shrink even more, and she let him be in charge. Sofia tried to force herself to believe it would get better.

Several weeks passed. One day Sofia had leaned her crutches against the hut wall and was sweeping the yard. She was keeping her balance by leaning on the broom.

Suddenly somebody snatched it away. Sofia lost her balance and fell.

It was Isaias who had grabbed the broom. Sofia noticed that he hadn't been drinking, but he apparently thought he had done something funny, because he was laughing.

He threw the broom onto the ground beside her.

"That gave you a surprise, didn't it?" he said.

Sofia didn't reply. She took hold of the broom and got up. Then she continued to sweep.

That night she sat by the fire for a long time. She had decided to leave. She couldn't stay. She felt sorry for Alfredo, but she couldn't take him with her.

Where she would go, she didn't know. In the end, she decided to return to the city. Maybe there would be someone there who could help her. If that didn't work, she would have to do what so many others did: sit down on the street and beg. Whatever happened, it would be better than staying here.

She was going to leave early, at dawn. She didn't have any money, so she would have to walk to the city. She didn't know if she would make it. Maybe the straps that held her legs to her body would break? Then she would have no choice but to crawl.

Even so, she didn't hesitate. She was going to the city. Doctor Raul was there. He would be able to help her.

She never went into the hut that night, but sat by the fire and watched it die. The night was warm and she snoozed against the wall of the hut. Then she went. She didn't look back as she left the village.

It took her three days and nights to get back to the city. Most of the way she limped along on her crutches, but from time to time a car would stop and give her a lift. Someone gave her a piece of bread. She drank water from pumps in the villages she passed.

On the second day, she discovered a crack in her left leg. That frightened her. She didn't want to meet Doctor Raul without her legs. She tried to put as much weight as possible on her right leg. It gave her a cramp and she had to stop more often.

Sofia arrived in the city late one evening. She crawled under a rusty, dismantled truck to sleep and wait for dawn. By then she was so hungry that her stomach ached. Big rats scrabbled around her. Now and then she tried to hit them with one of her crutches. She had never experienced such a long night. It was as if the sun had decided never to rise above the horizon again. She remembered what Muazena had described as the worst of all disasters: to be left alone. To be the last person on earth. Was she that person? Sofia Alface, underneath a rusty truck on the outskirts of a large city, somewhere in Africa?

Dawn finally arrived. She crawled out from under the truck and continued towards the city. After several hours, she had made her way to the hospital. In the car park she found Doctor Raul's car, with its bumper still hanging from a wire.

Sofia sat down against the car and waited.

That was where Doctor Raul found her at dusk, on his way home after a long day at the hospital.

CHAPTER TEN

DOCTOR RAUL'S WIFE was called Dolores. Although he loved her, and although they had four children together, he was also sometimes afraid of her. She could be very strict. He knew it irritated her that he was so absentminded. He also suspected that she was sometimes annoyed because he said they couldn't afford a new car.

This particular day, he was worried about what she would say when he brought Sofia home.

Sofia had been sitting asleep against his car when he left work. At first he'd thought she was one of the many street children who washed his car with their dirty rags, hoping he would give them some money. He'd already started digging through one of his pockets when he realized it was his former patient Sofia who was sitting beside one of the back wheels—the girl he'd driven home to the village outside Boane just a short while ago.

He stopped with a frown, knowing immediately that something was wrong. She must have heard him, or sensed he was there, because she opened her eyes. Doctor Raul did as he had done so many times before, when she'd been lying in her bed in the hospital. He crouched down in front of her.

"What's happened?" he asked.

"I couldn't stay at home," Sofia answered.

Doctor Raul let her answer sink in. Why hadn't she been able to stay? It sounded strange. African families never rejected anyone, no matter how poor they were, nor how distantly related the returning relative was who claimed a place by the fire.

Finally he did the only thing he could do. He sat on the ground beside her and leaned back against the car.

"Tell me about it," he said. "Tell me what happened."

Sofia's words came out in jerks, as if she was forcing them out in great pain.

She told the doctor about Isaias, how he'd come out of the darkness and how he'd pulled the broom out of her hand so that she fell.

Doctor Raul listened and knew that what she was telling him was probably true. She could have been exaggerating, of course, as children often did—especially poor children, whose only abundance was in the exaggeration of their despair. But it wasn't the first time he had heard such a story. Sofia's experience was common to an infinite number of children. One of the worst aspects of poverty and misery was that they forced people to do things against their will. Lydia no doubt needed a man to help her. But once the man was there, she had to obey him. And men often didn't want anything to do with the children women had from previous marriages. That could be particularly true with a girl like Sofia, a girl who'd had her legs blown away and who depended on crutches.

As he listened to the rest of Sofia's story, he gradually got a picture of what had happened. Sofia had returned to the city because she couldn't stay in the village with her mother. And the only person she could turn to was the doctor who had healed her.

Sofia was still his patient, he thought. He couldn't leave her here on the street. That would pretty soon be the end of her. She would be bullied and chased, beaten and abused by other children and adults who lived on the streets. Her crutches would be stolen, and so would her legs. They would show up somewhere else in the city, at a market where someone would offer them for sale. She'd starve and fall ill—from scabies, from the cough, from malaria. One day, she'd be lying dead underneath a filthy cardboard box. No one would know who she was. She'd be buried in one of the large graves that were regularly dug on the outskirts of the churchyards, the graves for the poor, where bodies were thrown down, without a coffin, without a priest, without anything—just as people throw rubbish into a bin outside their house in the morning.

He thought about his wife Dolores and wondered what she would say when he came home with Sofia.

But there wasn't anything else he could do.

"You must come home with me," he said. "Then we'll decide."

This time the car started without anyone having to push it.

Doctor Raul lived in a two-storey house. His home was on the ground floor. The house had a little garden. Hidden away behind some trees at the far end of the garden there was a shed where his night guard Sulemane lived. When Doctor Raul had problems, he would often talk to Sulemane about them. Sulemane was old and wise, though he wasn't a very good night guard because he would lie beside the gate sleeping when he was supposed to be awake. Several times, Doctor Raul had had to wake him when he arrived home late in the car. Dolores was angry with him for not firing Sulemane and hiring a night guard who would at least stay awake. But Doctor Raul didn't want to lose Sulemane—especially since he gave such good advice.

As they were driving home, he decided to talk to Sulemane about Sofia. Maybe he could advise what should be done.

Doctor Raul left Sofia sitting in the car while he went inside to tell Dolores he had brought one of his patients home with him.

"She could have slept at the hospital," Dolores said. "Why did you have to bring her home?"

"She needs a bath," Doctor Raul said. "She's filthy. I don't think you realize how far she's hopped on those crutches."

Dolores didn't say anything else, so Doctor Raul went outside to fetch Sofia. When Dolores saw Sofia, her irritation faded immediately. The girl really was filthy. And she looked exhausted and miserable.

"Poor child," she murmured. "Why does life have to be so hard?" She gave Sofia some food. Doctor Raul's children watched, curious. Sofia looked down self-consciously. The food was unfamiliar, but she was very hungry. She wasn't used to eating with a spoon because she usually ate with her fingers, but she thought she had better do what the others were doing.

After the meal, Dolores ran her a bath. When Sofia went into the bathroom she was speechless. She'd never seen a bathroom before. It was bigger than her whole house in the village. Shining and glossy, with running water, electric lighting, towels, and scented soaps. She couldn't see a fire anywhere but, even so, the water was hot. Dolores showed her what to do, then left her alone. Sofia undressed, unstrapped her legs, and lifted herself over the edge of the bathtub into the hot water. Never before had she experienced anything so wonderful.

She closed her eyes and thought about the ocean. The salt water hadn't been this warm, but she imagined herself floating on the waves and she drifted gradually off to sleep. When Dolores peeked in, Sofia was asleep, her head leaning against the edge of the tub. Dolores looked at her. The leg-stumps showed clearly in the water. She shook her head, then carefully woke Sofia.

"You were sleeping," she said. "Have a wash now, while the water is still warm."

Afterwards, when Sofia had dried herself, put her legs back on, and gotten dressed, Doctor Raul came to get her.

"It's time for you to sleep," he said. "Tomorrow we'll talk about what you should do."

"I can't stay at home," Sofia said again.

Doctor Raul nodded.

"We'll talk about it tomorrow," he said. "Not now."

Sofia lay in a bed in Doctor Raul's office—a room full of books with a large table covered in documents and newspapers. Light from the street shone through the window. She could hear voices in the distance. It was Dolores and Doctor Raul talking to each other. It made her feel safe. Although she was alone in the room with the books, there were people close by. She closed her eyes and pushed aside all thoughts. She was soon asleep.

Dolores and Doctor Raul were drinking coffee and discussing what they could do for Sofia.

"She has to go back home," Dolores said. "We can't solve her problem."

Doctor Raul knew his wife was right. But he also doubted Sofia would follow that advice. She had walked all the way from Boane, hobbling on her crutches in the unbearable heat, and she hadn't given in. He realized that her inner strength—the strength that had initially helped her to survive, and that now showed its will in refusing to live with a stepfather who laughed when she fell—was greater than he had thought.

Doctor Raul put down the coffee mug.

"I'm going out to talk to Sulemane," he said.

"She can stay here for a couple of days," Dolores said. "But not longer."

Sulemane was sitting by the gate mending his shoes. He was barely visible in the darkness. Doctor Raul had brought a garden chair with him, and he sat down. The night was warm. He told Sulemane about Sofia, while Sulemane sat calmly working. The soles had come loose and he was using a small hammer to knock in the tiny nails. Doctor Raul wondered how he managed to see anything at all in the darkness.

When Doctor Raul had finished his story, they sat in silence. The only sound was of Sulemane's hammer. Doctor Raul knew Sulemane was thinking over what he'd said. He wouldn't speak until he'd made up his mind.

An hour passed. Sulemane went on fixing his shoes. Doctor Raul waited.

When the shoes were finished, Sulemane spoke.

"Sooner or later her mother will come for her," he said. "Until then, there is nothing we can do."

"How long until that happens?"

"It may take a week. Or a month."

"But she can't stay here that long."

This was a new problem. Sulemane thought about it, and Doctor Raul waited.

"Sofia can stay with my sister Hermengarda," Sulemane said after some time. "My sister has a house between the church and the vegetable market."

Doctor Raul thought that was a good suggestion. The market was not too far away. If Sulemane said Sofia could stay with his sister, then that was that.

"I'll pay for her, of course," Doctor Raul said.

Sulemane didn't answer. Doctor Raul knew that he was working out how much money he thought his sister should get. But Doctor Raul didn't need to wait around for that answer. He'd get it the following morning. He returned to the house and told Dolores what Sulemane had said.

"Maybe she will come and fetch her daughter," she answered. "Let's hope Sulemane is right."

"He's rarely wrong," Doctor Raul said.

They went to bed. Before he switched off the lights, Doctor Raul went to his office. Sofia's head was dark against the white pillow. He stood for a while watching her sleep. Then he crept off to his own bed.

"A remarkable girl," Dolores said.

"No one who meets her forgets her," Doctor Raul said.

Sofia moved in with Sulemane's sister Hermengarda. The house was small and many people lived there. As far as Hermengarda was concerned, it made no difference if another person joined the family. She was large and strong and sold live hens at the market. Every morning, Sofia was woken at dawn by a raucous cackling outside the house. Hermengarda was discussing chicken prices with the buyers. Sofia shared her bed with a girl called Louisa. There was no bathroom in Hermengarda's house, but Sofia felt more at home there than at Doctor Raul's. She helped to clean and tidy up and look after the youngest children. But she didn't forget that she needed to think about the future. She was only living at Hermengarda's temporarily. Sofia secretly hoped that Lydia would soon turn up outside Hermengarda's house and tell her that Isaias had gone and that she could come home. But she was angry with Lydia, as well, and felt as if she had been traded for a mean man who would never be of any use. She worried about Alfredo, who was all on his own.

If only I had Maria to talk to, she thought. The only thing I've got now is the fire in Hermengarda's fireplace. I need Muazena's help.

Soon after Sofia moved in, Hermengarda asked whether there was anything Sofia liked to do.

"To sew," Sofia immediately replied.

Hermengarda nodded.

"That's good," she answered. "I'll see what I can do."

The next day, Hermengarda woke Sofia early in the morning, even before the man with the cackling hens had arrived.

"Get dressed," she said. "Hurry up. I have a good friend with a small sewing studio. She's promised to let you show her what you can do. If she thinks you're capable, you can work there. You won't get paid, but you'll be trained. That's more important than money."

Sofia strapped on her legs and dressed as quickly as she could. Hermengarda, who always had lots to do, was already waiting impatiently on the street. When Sofia was ready they hurried off.

Hermengarda walked so fast that Sofia almost had to run on her crutches. But it wasn't far. Before long, Hermengarda stopped outside a tumbledown house hidden in an overgrown garden. The drainpipes had fallen off and there were cracks in the concrete stairs.

The door was open and Hermengarda shouted for someone called Fatima. A woman, just as black and just as big as Hermengarda, came out onto the steps.

"Here I am with Sofia," Hermengarda said. "I don't have time to stay."

Then she turned to Sofia.

"You'll find your way back home again this afternoon, won't you?"

Sofia was sure she would be able to manage that. Hermengarda disappeared and Sofia was alone with Fatima, who stood on the steps squinting at her from behind a pair of glasses.

"Come closer so I can have a look at you," she said.

Sofia hopped carefully towards Fatima. When she came to the stairs Fatima turned around, beckoning to Sofia to follow her inside. Sofia heaved herself up the steps on her crutches.

When she entered the house, it was like stepping into a completely different world. The whole house was filled with birds. Cages hung everywhere: big, small, square, round, cages made of wood, of grass, of fabric. Everywhere there was a chirping and screeching of colorful birds. Sofia stood stunned in the doorway. There were even birds flying around in the room.

A glittering silver pigeon alighted on her shoulder and started pulling at her hair. Fatima had disappeared into an adjacent room, but came back to see where Sofia had got to.

"You're not scared of birds, are you?" she asked. "You can't work for me if you are."

Sofia shook her head. She wasn't afraid of birds. It was just astonishing to enter a house where there were more birds than people.

"I've always dreamed about waking up one morning with wings on my back," Fatima said. "It will probably never happen. So I surround myself with birds instead. Thousands of wings flapping and fluttering and rising towards the gray and blue skies."

She beckoned Sofia to follow her into the next room. It was large and round and had tall windows around the walls. Sofia had never been inside such a large and light room before. In the middle stood a big sewing table with several sewing machines. Along the walls there were shelves with different-colored fabrics. Dolls, as big as people, stood in various parts of the room. Fabric and half-finished dresses hung on the dolls. They looked at Sofia with glassy eyes.

Fatima laughed.

"When you've stopped gaping, you can sit down at this bench," she said, pointing. "Then we can get to work."

When Sofia met Fatima, it was just as if she had met Muazena's sister. Although she was younger and stouter than Muazena, Fatima was as full of the same hidden strength as Muazena had been. She told stories and explained things as she sewed in the same manner that Muazena would stubbornly hoe the soil or pull weeds while she talked. Time seemed to stand still during the period Sofia spent with Fatima, among the birds and the fabric they transformed into clothes.

Fatima was a strict teacher. She was angry when Sofia was neglectful or didn't do what she had been told. But Sofia noticed that she never raised her voice or sighed and complained without reason. And she always praised Sofia when she did something well.

Above all, she taught Sofia the secrets of the sewing needle.

One evening they were working late, even though it was already dark. They were working on a white silk wedding dress that had to be ready the next day. Fatima had promised Sofia that she could stay the night when they were finished. She had hired a boy to clean out the birdcages, and she sent him over to Hermengarda with the message that Sofia would not be back until the following day.

It grew late. The evening had turned into night by the time the white dress was finally ready. Fatima nodded happily and put an arm around Sofia's shoulders.

"It can't get any better than this," she said.

Then they had tea on the verandah. The birds were

quiet in their cages, and a light breeze wafted through the silence.

Fatima and Sofia sat next to each other on a swinging sofa, balancing their cracked cups in their hands.

"It was an old man who taught me how to sew," Fatima said suddenly. Her voice was low, as if she didn't want to disturb the silence.

"He taught me that everything in life is about scams," she continued. "Seams bind things together. There are invisible seams between people. Our dreams use our waking thoughts to stitch our memories firmly to us. If you want to be wise and learn about people, you should sew. If you embroider your longings and sorrows onto a piece of fabric, you will soon feel your burdens growing lighter."

That was what Fatima told Sofia that night. And Sofia never forgot it. The very next day, she started sewing together two leftover pieces of fabric. One of them was Maria, and the other one was herself. She embroidered a design of different-colored threads to form the name "Lydia," which meant that she missed her mother. She embroidered a road, which meant that she waited every day for Lydia to come and tell her that Isaias was gone and that she could come home.

From that night, she knew that sewing was what she wanted to do in life. And when Fatima began praising her more often, and giving her more advanced things to do, she started believing that she would be able to do it.

Time passed. Lydia didn't come to get her. Every day, Sofia hoped that Doctor Raul would knock at Hermengarda's door to say that Lydia had been looking for her at the hospital. But he never had any news of Lydia. She didn't come. Doctor Raul noticed that Sofia was growing sad, and so he told her instead how happy he was that she had become so good at sewing.

Sofia tried not to think about Lydia, Alfredo, and Faustino, though it was hard. She had brought home the two pieces of fabric that represented Maria and herself. Whenever she had difficulties sleeping, she got out of bed and worked on her sewing by the gleam of the streetlights. Gradually, it made things feel easier. But the longing was always there. Why didn't Lydia come? Had she forgotten she had a daughter called Sofia?

The wet season pulled in over the city. It rained nonstop for days and weeks. The city filled with so much water that the streets were almost invisible. But every morning Sofia went over to Fatima and the birds' house. And every night she returned to Hermengarda's.

One evening as the rain poured down, someone knocked at the door. It was Doctor Raul. Sofia leaped

out of her chair. At last he'd come to tell her that
Lydia had been looking for her at the hospital. She
gazed at him with anticipation as he stood dripping
rain on the floor from his face and clothes.

"A man came to the hospital today asking for you,"
he said.

Sofia went cold inside. It must have been Isaias.
Had he come to force her back home?

"It was an old man," Doctor Raul said.

She looked at him in confusion. Isaias wasn't old.
Who could it have been?

"He said his name was Totio," Doctor Raul said.
"And he'll be back tomorrow. He's coming here to
visit you."

Totio? The man with the sewing machine? What
could he want with her?

Sofia slept poorly that night. And the next day
she was so sloppy with the seams that Fatima wondered whether she was ill. But Sofia was just waiting for Totio. She could hardly wait to find out what
he wanted.

Then Totio arrived.

Late that evening, he knocked at the door of
Hermengarda's house.

CHAPTER ELEVEN

WHEN SOFIA SAW old Totio standing in the rain outside Hermengarda's house, she was so happy that she surprised herself. She'd only known Totio briefly, and yet he had come to visit her. She tried to read his wrinkled face for a clue to what he wanted. Hermengarda invited him to come inside instead of standing out in the rain, but Totio refused. It was already late. He was staying with relatives in a suburb far away and he still had a long way to walk.

"I just wanted to see that Sofia was here," he said. "If it's all right, I was hoping to visit her tomorrow."

Hermengarda gave him the directions to Fatima's house. Then Totio lifted his ragged old hat and disappeared into the darkness.

"Who was that?" Hermengarda asked.

"Totio," Sofia answered. "He's got a sewing machine."

Sofia was annoyed with him for not having told her what he wanted. He wouldn't have traveled all the way to the city just to ask her how she was. It couldn't have been Lydia who sent him, either. They didn't even know each other.

She slept restlessly and dreamed that Totio was lost in the city and would never return.

When she woke up at dawn, it was still raining. But Hermengarda was in a hurry as usual, and was cranky with Sofia for being slow. Sofia pulled a plastic bag over her hair, wrapped an old *capulana* around her body and hobbled along in the water that had risen high on the streets. She was splashed with water several times by careless drivers.

When she arrived at Fatima's house, there was a surprise waiting for her. Totio had already arrived. He was sheltering from the rain under a tree. Sofia hoped Fatima wouldn't mind that a man, one who also owned a sewing machine and knew the secrets of thread and fabric, had come to visit her.

"You shouldn't stand here in the rain, Uncle Totio," she said. "We'll go inside."

Sofia pushed the door open and they went in. The birds were flapping and cheeping everywhere. Totio was just as stunned as Sofia had been the first time she came to Fatima's house. He looked around in amazement.

"*A phsi nyenhana a ku shonga,*" Totio said. "What beautiful birds."

"*Ina,*" Sofia agreed, and smiled.

Fatima was busy cutting a piece of fabric for a blouse when Sofia came in with Totio. They greeted one another and started chatting right away. Fatima told him to take off his wet clothes and wrap a blanket around himself, but Totio said he was all right. However, he gently dried off his ragged hat and laid it carefully on a chair.

Then, for the rest of the day, he sat on the chair beside the hat and watched Sofia work. He still hadn't mentioned why he had come. Sofia knew that old people often took a long time to ask a question or relate a piece of news. Now that Totio had arrived, she would have to wait. But when the afternoon arrived, and he had still done nothing other than closely follow Sofia's work, she began to feel impatient. Why didn't he say anything?

It seemed he was particularly interested in watching her sew on Fatima's machines. Sofia felt proud that she made no mistakes while Totio was there.

It wasn't until they were finishing their work for the day that Totio finally spoke up. Fatima had disappeared into the kitchen and was banging saucepans around when Sofia suddenly heard his voice.

"I see that you can now sew," he said. "You've already learned how to use a sewing machine. It was to see this that I came."

Sofia sat listening with her hands on her thighs.

"I've grown old," Totio continued. "My eyesight is very poor. I don't want to sew my seams so sloppily that my customers will start complaining. For that reason, I have decided to stop sewing. Fernanda and I are moving back to Mueda. I've come here to ask if you would like to take over my hut and my sewing machine."

Sofia thought she had heard wrongly.

"I don't have any money to pay you," she said.

"I thought you could send us money when you had some to spare," Totio said. "We old folks don't need too much."

Sofia was still wondering whether there was something she hadn't understood. Did Totio mean that he would give her his sewing machine? That she would take over the job as seamstress and tailor in the village outside Boane?

Totio understood her surprise.

"I haven't made this long journey to tell you something that isn't true," he continued.

Sofia realized he meant what he was saying. Thoughts flitted around in her head like the birds in Fatima's house.

"I can't," she said.

"Why can't you?"

Sofia told him about Isaias—about why she had returned to the city. When she was finished, Totio nodded long and slowly.

"I understand how it could be difficult," he said. "But you have to remember that you can take over my and Fernanda's hut. You'll be working and taking care of yourself. You would only see Isaias when you wanted to see him."

"Never," Sofia said.

"That might well be. You can decide that for yourself."

He got up with some difficulty and put the old hat back on his head. His gray hair showed through the broken brim.

"I have seen that you can sew," he said again. "You've still got a lot to learn, but now I can return and tell Fernanda that Sofia will be able to take over the sewing machine. That will make the road home shorter."

He came across and put his hand on her shoulder.

"You're not going to stay here in the city," he said. "You're just visiting. You belong to the village. You know now that you have something to return to. Come back in a couple of weeks. Don't be too long."

Then he left.

Sofia stood by the window and watched him disappear into the rain. She had no doubt that it was Muazena who had sent him to her.

She pressed her face against the foggy glass. At that moment she missed Maria more than ever.

Suddenly Fatima was standing beside her. Sofia hadn't heard her come.

"Did what he said make you happy or sad?" she asked.

"I don't know," Sofia answered.

"I didn't hear everything," Fatima said, "but I agree with him that you are a good seamstress. I think you should return to your village. That's where you belong. Not here."

That night, Sofia sat huddled for a long time in a corner of the bed in Hermengarda's house, thinking about what Totio had said. She could already imagine herself on the bench in the shade of the tree, eagerly treadling the black sewing machine. The thread would run, the needle would make its straight and even seams, customers would nod contentedly, and others would wait in line to ask her about one thing and another. But the image disappeared as soon as she thought about Isaïas. How could she live in the same village as Lydia, when Lydia had given up her own daughter in favor of a mean man who drank *tontonto*? It would be so difficult that it would ruin the joy of Totio's sewing machine.

She remembered something Muazena had said a long, long time ago: *Without your family, you are nothing.*

That was what she had said. And Sofia knew she was right. Disappointed as she was in Lydia, her longing was greater. She missed Lydia every single day.

The days passed without Sofia being able to make up her mind. Fatima asked her but she replied evasively and bent over her work. On Sunday, she went to visit Doctor Raul and Dolores. They were happy to see her. She told them about Totio's visit, but when she came to the hard part and tried to explain to them how much she missed Lydia, she mumbled and went silent.

"When are you going home?" Doctor Raul asked. "If you dare to ride with me one more time, I'll drive you."

"I don't know," Sofia answered.

"Let us know a couple of days beforehand," Dolores said. "I think I would like to come along, too."

Sofia returned to Hermengarda's house. She was annoyed with herself for having mumbled. But she was also angry with Doctor Raul and Dolores for not understanding how difficult it was going to be to return to her hometown, knowing her family was there and yet not wanting to see them.

It's not going to work, she thought. Totio is going to get tired of waiting for me. He's going to give the sewing machine to someone else.

Monday came. Sofia woke and heard the rain thundering on the tin roof. She didn't want to get up, and pulled her sheet above her head. She could hear Hermengarda out in the kitchen and knew she would soon come in and yell at her for not being up and dressed. Then she heard someone knocking at the front door, and heard Hermengarda call, "Come in." Sofia supposed it was one of the chicken suppliers wanting their money. She pressed her hands over her ears so she wouldn't have to listen to the cackling hens, squeezed her eyes shut, and tried to go back to sleep.

Then someone tugged at the sheet over her head. Hermengarda had come to scold her, of course.

But then she noticed it wasn't Hermengarda's hand.

She opened her eyes and pulled the sheet aside.

And looked straight into Lydia's face.

It wasn't a dream. It really was Lydia. She smiled. And the teeth that had fallen out of her mouth were still missing.

"Sofia," said Lydia. "Is it really you?"

Sofia nodded.

Lydia sat on the floor beside the bed. She had Faustino with her, and he was crying where he hung against Lydia's back. She started breast-feeding him. Sofia pulled herself down onto the floor and strapped her legs on. Then she got dressed.

Faustino fell asleep again. Lydia handed him to Sofia,

who took him into her arms. He looked like Alfredo.

"You can come back home," Lydia said. "Isaias is no longer there."

Sofia sat holding Faustino while she listened to Lydia.

"Isaias wasn't a good man," she said. "He had plenty to say, but it was never connected to what he did. Last week he broke into José-Maria's place and stole a box of money. Someone saw him but when the police came from Boane to question him, he denied everything. It was Alfredo who found the box with the money. Isaias had buried it behind the old hen cage. When Alfredo arrived carrying the box, Isaias had no choice but to admit to stealing the money. The police took him away with them. He knows that he can never return to us when they release him from prison."

Lydia spoke with downcast eyes as if she were ashamed in front of Sofia, even though Sofia was her daughter. The anger and grief Sofia had been carrying were suddenly gone. Now she just felt sorry for Lydia, who had grown so old and tired since they had been forced to flee the burned village.

But now nothing was difficult anymore. Sofia could go back home. And she could accept Totio's sewing machine. But she had a question for Muazena, which she would ask her the next time she saw her face among the flames. Sofia needed to know how, when things were difficult and hard to bear, so much time could pass without anything happening. And then, how everything would suddenly happen at once. Muazena would surely have an answer for her.

"I had planned to visit Maria's grave," Lydia said suddenly. "But maybe you won't be able to come? I understand that you have a job."

Sofia had never thought she would ever visit Maria's grave.

"I'll ask Fatima," she said. "We can go together. But I don't know where Maria's grave is."

"Once we get to the big cemetery by the river, I'll remember how to find it."

They went to Fatima's house. Lydia didn't want to come inside because she was ashamed of her plain clothes. Sofia went in and asked Fatima if she could be allowed to visit her sister's grave with her mother. Fatima was almost angry with Sofia for having asked.

"Of course you can visit the cemetery," she said. She even gave Sofia some money so that they wouldn't have to walk all the way through the city to get there. Then she explained how Sofia could find a truck that would take them in the right direction.

Lydia seemed to be afraid of the city. She kept close to Sofia to shield herself from the tall buildings, the cars, and the people who all seemed to be in such a hurry. They arrived at the cemetery in an old recon-ditioned jeep. Lydia thought for a long time before she indicated the direction they should walk in.

The cemetery was vast. Its rusted gates hung from cracked concrete posts. Just inside the gates there were small buildings with crosses on them, and in-side these there were stone coffins stacked one on top of the other. On each tomb was carved the names of the families who kept their dead there. Sofia was horrified to see that poor people, who had nowhere else to live, had moved into the tombs. They slept and cooked their food between the coffins. It gave her the creeps to think that she herself might one day be so poor that she would be forced to live in a tomb.

They walked further and arrived at long rows of white headstones. Many of them had faded and fallen apart. Lizards ran about among the dried flowers and broken crosses. The cemetery seemed endless. At last the headstones became fewer and they arrived at a wide field where plain wooden crosses were all that marked where the dead lay buried. Lydia stopped and looked around, then they continued on. It wasn't until they reached the outskirts of the cemetery that they found what they were looking for.

"Here it is," Lydia said and wiped the sweat from her face with her head-cloth.

Sofia looked around, but she couldn't see a grave.

"Many people lie buried together," Lydia said.

"People who were just as poor as we are. But I know this is the place."

They sat in the shade of a tall tree. Sofia tried to imagine that Maria was somewhere nearby, buried in the ground. At the same time she decided that the first money she earned would be spent buying Maria a cross. Not until then would she fully accept that this was where Maria had been buried.

Lydia began to shake. A long howl broke from her. Sofia began rocking as well and, before long, she found herself wailing.

They sat together for hours, mourning Maria.

It wasn't until the sun had sunk towards the horizon that Sofia suggested they think about going back. She had enough money for another truck.

Lydia slept on the floor in Sofia's room that night. Sofia had wanted to give her the bed, but Lydia stubbornly refused. She curled up on a straw mat beside the bed with Faustino pressed against her body. The next morning she left. José-Maria had promised her a ride on a truck back to the village. Sofia explained to her where to find the market where the trucks were.

"Come home soon," Lydia said as they made their goodbyes outside Hermengarda's house.

Sofia still hadn't mentioned Totio's visit and his offer of the hut and the sewing machine. She first needed to be sure that it wasn't already too late. After that she could return to the village. But until then, she couldn't tell Lydia.

She waved to Lydia and watched her disappear around a street corner. Then she hurried to Fatima's house where the birds and the fabric were waiting for her.

Sofia never needed to ask Totio. He returned to the city himself to ask if she'd made up her mind.

He came with Fernanda about a week after Lydia had visited Sofia. When Sofia answered that she would love to take over the sewing machine, big fat Fernanda danced with joy. Fatima's birds were startled and flew in all directions.

"We are going to celebrate this," Fernanda said and took Totio's broken hat from him. "We are going to celebrate by buying you a new hat."

Totio didn't say anything. Sofia got the feeling that he would rather have kept wearing his old hat, broken and dirty though it was.

They decided that Sofia would stay with Fatima for another month. Then she would return to the village.

Sofia's last day of work at Fatima's was over. In her spare time, Sofia had embroidered a small tablecloth for Fatima. On a piece of blue fabric, which she imagined as a piece of the sky, she had embroidered the birds that flew around in their cages and around her head. She gave the tablecloth to Fatima when they parted. Sofia felt shy and kept her eyes lowered as she handed her the present. Fatima looked at it and exclaimed with pleasure.

"How beautiful it is," she cried. "This will always remind me of the time you spent here."

Then she took the needle out of the sewing machine Sofia had worked with.

"Take it with you," she said and gave it to Sofia. "Then you'll remember Fatima and all her birds."

The next day, Doctor Raul and Dolores came to Hermengarda's house to pick her up. Sofia promised that she would come and visit Hermengarda as often as she could.

The rain stopped on the day they left the city. Sofia sat in the backseat and she rolled the window down to let the wind blow on her face. Now she was no longer afraid to return home.

When they arrived, Lydia and Alfredo were standing outside the hut.

For a brief moment, Sofia almost expected Maria to come running to meet her.

Then she remembered that Maria only existed inside her.

But she felt as if she'd finally come home.

CHAPTER TWELVE

SOFIA WAS UP before Lydia woke.

She crawled carefully over Alfredo, fetched her legs from where they leaned against the wall, and went out past the straw mat hanging across the doorway.

Outside it was still dark. Sofia strapped her legs on, first the left one, and then the right. She suddenly remembered she'd forgotten to bring the crutches from the hut. She got up, took hold of the hut wall and pulled the straw mat aside. She tried to be as quiet as possible, because she wanted to be gone before Lydia woke up. She fumbled around for the crutches. Then she let the straw mat fall back in its place and headed off through the darkness. The first light of dawn was not yet visible in the sky. It had rained during the night. The road was still hard, which made the going easier for her, but when the wet season arrived it would turn the roads into waterlogged mud. Sofia knew she would have difficulties getting around when that happened. The crutches would get stuck in the mud, and she could easily lose her balance.

She got to the open space in front of the school, where she turned right. By then she could see the pink of morning in the eastern sky. Somewhere close by a cock crowed, and a goat bleated in reply.

There was always a strong smell just after rain. She breathed in the fresh air. It reminded her of the village where she had lived with Maria and Muazena and Hapakatanda.

She hadn't forgotten the promise she and Maria had made each other. One day they would return to the village where Muazena's and Hapakatanda's spirits lived on and waited for them.

Now she would have to return without Maria.

But it would still feel as though Maria was with her.

Totio was already up and sitting on the wooden bench beside the sewing machine when Sofia came hopping along on her crutches. Sofia felt a little uneasy. What if he had changed his mind?

When she went up to him, he nodded and made room on the bench so she could sit down. Neither of them said a word. Sofia stole a glance at Totio. He seemed to be absorbed in his own thoughts. The sewing machine was covered by its brown wooden lid. From inside the hut came the penetrating sound of Fernanda snoring.

"The day will always come when life changes," Totio said suddenly. "You know it's going to happen, but it's still a surprise."

He leaned across the table and removed the wooden cover. Then he ran his hand over the black machine.

"I've been using this machine for thirty-five years," he said. "How many spools of thread have run through the needle into trousers, dresses, shirts, and caps, I don't know. But the thread has run through my life. And now it's over."

Sofia could tell that Totio was sad. She guessed it was probably difficult to grow old and not be able to work anymore.

But she didn't ask if that was why he was sad. She didn't say anything. The sun was already up.

Totio bent down and picked up something that had been lying under the bench. He gave it to Sofia. It was a square piece of hard, white cardboard. Someone had written on it SEWING STUDIO. OWNER: SOFIA ALFACE.

"When you arrive tomorrow, the sign will be up," Totio said. "When you come, my sign will be gone. And we will be gone, Fernanda and I. The hut is yours. And the sewing machine. And all the customers."

Sofia felt her heart beat faster. She was sweating with excitement.

So it really was true after all. She was going to take over the machine and the hut. Tomorrow.

"Always remember that satisfied customers will come back," Totio said. "Unhappy customers will come only once and then never return."

"There are so many things I still need to learn," Sofia said.

"That goes for me too," Totio said. "You never learn everything."

The snoring from inside the hut had stopped. Soon Fernanda appeared. She yawned and knotted her *capulana* around her big body.

"I think you should know it was Fernanda's suggestion," Totio said. "When I realized my eyes weren't able to see anymore, I said I was going to sell the sewing machine. But Fernanda thought it better that you continue the work, and send us money from time to time."

Fernanda sat down on the bench. Sofia was squashed between her and Totio.

"A sewing machine is for sewing," Fernanda said. "You shouldn't sell it."

"I don't know how to thank you," Sofia said with embarrassment.

"You're not going to thank us," Fernanda said. "You are going to sew."

Sofia stayed with Totio and Fernanda the whole day. She helped them pack. They were going to leave early the next day. First they would go up to the main road with their bags and baskets. Then they would catch a bus and travel for many days to distant Mueda, where they had lived before. During the day, many people from the village came to say goodbye. Totio talked the whole time about what a good seamstress Sofia was, saying they should come to her when they needed something made or mended.

They said goodbye late in the afternoon.

"I've spoken to a boy who is going to watch the sewing machine tonight," Totio said. "No one will steal it."

And that was it. Fernanda patted Sofia's cheek, Totio took her hand in his. It was creased, but strong. He held her hand for a long time.

Sofia hobbled home on her crutches. She was going to miss them a lot.

After they'd eaten that night, Lydia stayed outside. Sofia could tell there was something Lydia wanted to talk about. The fire was burning and Sofia looked into her mother's face. Though Lydia was still young, she seemed tired and weary. It was as if she'd already grown old, although she should still have been able to bear many more children.

"I don't have many words," she said. "But I have many thoughts. When I saw you and Maria on that path I thought my life was over. Everything had been taken away from me: my husband, Hapakatanda, my village, my children. But you survived, and now you have your own home and a sewing machine. You have two new legs and people in the village speak of you with respect. I believe that both Hapakatanda and Maria are watching you. And they are just as proud as I am."

"Don't forget Muazena," Sofia said.

"She was a witch," Lydia said. "I was scared of her."

"I wasn't," Sofia said. "And neither was Maria."

"In any case, I wanted you to know that I'm proud of you," Lydia said. "Through you, I have been able to hold on to some of my happiness."

Sofia had never heard Lydia speak like this to her before. It felt strange, but it made her happy.

Lydia went to bed. Sofia had already packed her few belongings, so she remained by the fire. She soon could tell that Lydia had fallen asleep.

Sofia sat looking into the flames. This time she could see all the faces clearly. Hapakatanda was there. Muazena was there. Maria was there. Sofia suddenly saw herself as a very small girl. She was being held high above the ground and Hapakatanda was showing her the sun. Maybe it didn't matter whether you were alive or dead. You still belonged to the same family.

She understood, now, what the secrets in the fire were.

It was there, in the fire, that she could meet all those who belonged to her—whether they were alive or dead, whether they lived close by or far away. Everything could be found in the fire.

Sofia didn't know how long she stayed sitting by the fire. But several times she laid on more wood to make the flames blaze. This was the last night that she would sit by this particular fire. She would be leaving early the following morning. And that evening, she would light her own fire for the first time.

It was a big moment, an important moment.

She looked at her legs, her friends. They had a long way to walk, through many days and through many cycles of the moon.

Sofia got up early next morning. Lydia was already awake. They felt self-conscious as they said goodbye in front of the hut.

"We're living in the same village," Sofia said. "We won't be far from each other."

"Even so, I feel in my heart that you are moving away from us," Lydia said. "I need time to get used to that."

She gave Sofia a basket of tomatoes as a going-away present.

Sofia walked with a bundle on her head. It was difficult to keep it balanced, since she had to keep looking down to watch where to place the crutches. It took time, but it worked.

When she arrived, the first thing she saw was a sign on the tree next to the hut. SEWING STUDIO. OWNER: SOFIA ALFACE.

She had to take the bundle off her head to look at the sign properly. It shone in the sunlight.

Sofia Alface, she thought. That's me. No one else. Just me.

A boy was sitting next to the sewing machine. He came over to Sofia and helped her with the bundle. Sofia entered her new home. Fernanda had cleaned it, and everything was tidy and newly swept. Sofia sat on the squeaky bed and looked around. Apart from the bed, there were only two chairs and a rickety table. But the roof was intact and wouldn't leak. And the straw walls wouldn't need to be remade until next year.

This is Sofia Alface's house, she thought. The one who has taken over Totio's sewing machine.

She went outside and sat down by the sewing machine. She lifted off the wooden cover. Then she found a reel of thread, fastened it to the spool, and licked the end.

She got the thread through the eye of the needle on her first try.

She was ready. Now she could start working. Then she began to worry that no customers would come.

But they came. And the first was José-Maria.

When Sofia noticed him on the road she felt shy and didn't know what to say. What if he thought she was still too young to have her own sewing machine?

But José-Maria behaved just as he usually did. He pushed his glasses up onto his forehead and nodded at her.

"I have a pair of trousers that need mending," he said. "But I need them by tomorrow."

He gave her a parcel wrapped in newspaper. Sofia unwrapped it and spread out the black trousers. A seam had split. It would be easy to mend.

"I can do it immediately," she said.

"It's all right, so long as they're finished by tomorrow," José-Maria said. "Am I your first customer?"

Sofia blushed and nodded.

"I think this will go well for you, Sofia," he said. "But don't forget that you have to continue school. At least until you can read better, and write and do sums. I'll speak to Filomena. A couple of classes each day."

Sofia mended his pants as soon as he left. When she first started treadling the machine, she was afraid that it wouldn't obey her. Would it miss Totio? But nothing went wrong. The thread ran and the needle pricked as they were supposed to. Later, when José-Maria's trousers were ready, she couldn't help patting the machine, just as she'd seen Totio do.

The boy who'd been guarding the sewing machine during the night was sitting in the shade of a tree. He watched Sofia the whole time. Whenever she looked at him, he lowered his eyes.

"Who are you?" Sofia asked, when several hours had passed.

"Fabiao," the boy said.

"Why are you sitting here doing nothing?" Sofia

asked. "Why aren't you at school? Why aren't you watching the goats? Why are you just sitting down?"

Fabiao shrugged.

Sofia didn't have a chance to ask anything else. A woman arrived who wanted her dress let out.

"I've become so fat," she complained. "I can't get into my clothes anymore. Look at this dress. That's how thin I once was."

Sofia compared the dress to the woman who stood in front of her. Suddenly she found it difficult not to laugh. She had to bite her tongue to keep the laughter down. The woman looked at her in confusion.

"Can't you answer?" she asked angrily. "If it had been Totio, he would have started working on the dress right away. I don't understand how he could leave his sewing machine to someone with so little experience."

"I'll do it," Sofia said.

"If it doesn't look good, I won't pay," the woman said.

"It'll be good," Sofia replied. "It will be ready tomorrow."

"I'll have to see it before I believe it," the woman said and waddled away.

Once Sofia was on her own again, she couldn't help laughing. Then she began to work. The sun was already high in the sky. Sofia started letting out the dress. The boy under the tree had disappeared. Sofia worked for hour after hour. Even though her sweat ran, she barely gave herself a break for a drink of water. The village dozed in the afternoon heat, but Sofia worked on. The sewing machine whirred. The boy by the tree hadn't returned.

It was nearly dusk when Sofia noticed that she would not only manage to let out the dress, but she would do it so well that even the strict Totio would approve of the result. She decided to finish the work early the next morning, folded up the dress, and stretched her back. She hadn't eaten anything all day. She went into the hut and fetched some of the tomatoes she'd brought with her in the morning.

When she came out again, the boy had come back. He was standing next to the sewing machine.

"Don't touch it!" Sofia shouted.

"I wasn't going to," answered Fabiao. "I've got something for you."

Sofia threw down the crutches, swung across to the bench, and sat down.

The boy stood in front of her with a basket.

"There's a girl who wants you to sew a dress," he said.

He gave her the basket.

There was a large piece of white fabric in it.

Sofia felt the fabric. It was soft, almost like silk.

"Who is it that wants the dress?" she asked.

"She didn't tell me her name," Fabiao replied. "But she paid money in advance."

He put down a few banknotes on the table next to the sewing machine.

"I need to know how big the girl is," Sofia said. "I can't make a dress without knowing how big it's supposed to be."

"It would fit you," Fabiao said. "She said you were the same size."

Sofia suddenly felt strange. She put the fabric back in the basket.

"Who is this girl?" she asked.

"I don't know," Fabiao said. "It was an old woman who gave me the fabric and the money."

"When is the dress supposed to be ready?"

"Before the next full moon."

Sofia looked at Fabiao for a long time before she answered.

"Tell the old woman that I'll sew a white dress," she said. "A white dress that fits me."

Fabiao nodded and ran off. Dusk fell. Deep in thought, Sofia made up a fire. She was too tired to eat. She just sat on her straw mat and stared into the flames. She had put the wooden cover back on the sewing machine. Before she went to bed, she would carry it into the hut. No one was allowed to steal Totio's sewing machine.

The white fabric was in the basket beside her.

She knew that Muazena had come back. It was

Maria who was to have the dress. Maria who was dead, but who was still there, inside Sofia—or else deep in the fire that flickered in front of her.

Maria, who would always be there.

I'll make the dress, Sofia thought. I'll make it as beautifully as I can. And one day, when I have worked hard for a long time and have made enough money, I'll take Lydia and Alfredo and Faustino with me, and we'll return to the village that the bandits burned that night, so many full moons ago. And maybe I'll even see the ocean again.

She sat by the fire for a long time, deeply absorbed by the flames. She had removed her legs and laid them beside her. The tropical night was warm. Grasshoppers creaked, a dog barked in the distance. The starlit sky above her head was filled with unanswered questions.

Then she crawled into the hut with the sewing machine and her legs, let the straw mat fall across the door opening again, and went to sleep.

Outside the fire slowly faded.

The smouldering coals grew weaker.

Sofia slept.

On a path in her dreams, Maria ran towards her.

And the night, the African night, was still.

MESSAGE FROM
ADOPT-A-MINEFIELD

THE GLOBAL LANDMINE CRISIS is one of the most pervasive humanitarian problems facing the world today. It is estimated that there are between 60 and 70 million landmines in the ground in at least 70 countries. Approximately every 30 seconds, another innocent person is maimed or killed by a landmine. UNICEF estimates that 30%-40% of all mine victims are children under the age of 15. Survivors are forced to endure a lifetime of physical, psychological, and economic hardship.

LANDMINE REALITIES
- Landmines threaten life long after wars are over.
- Antipersonnel landmines are designed to maim and incapacitate. They are activated by the victim, rather than exploding on impact as other munitions do.
- Antipersonnel landmines cost as little as $3 to manufacture and $300 to $1,000 to remove.

- Most landmine survivors cannot afford to pay for proper care. Yet as little as $30 can help a child walk again.
- Children require a new prosthesis up to every six months, adults every three to five years.

ADOPT-A-MINEFIELD SERVES THREE MAIN PURPOSES
- To help save lives by raising funds to clear minefields.
- To provide assistance to landmine survivors.
- To raise awareness about the global landmine crisis.

You Can Be a Part of the Solution

Please join us as a steward of the environment in the global effort to end the terror of landmines and help make our Earth a safer place for each of us. With your help, we will clear a path to a safer world.

For further information, please visit the Adopt-A-Minefield website at www.landmines.org, e-mail info@landmines.org, or call (212) 907-1305.

ABOUT THE AUTHOR
AND THE TRANSLATOR

HENNING MANKELL is one of Sweden's best-selling authors. He has published a number of plays and novels for adults, many of them drawing on his experience in Africa. For children and young adults he writes poetic, intimate stories with strong narrative appeal, and these have won him several awards, including the prestigious Astrid Lindgren Prize.

Sofia, the heroine of *Secrets in the Fire*, is a real person, a friend of Henning Mankell's. Her moving story has been adapted for film.

ANNE CONNIE STUKSRUD was born in Norway but has lived and studied in Australia since 1996. She has published two short story collections for young adults in Scandinavia, and is currently working on her third book.